A NEW ME

A New Me

Edwin Roy Jones

Dernier Publishing
London

Text Copyright © Edwin Roy Jones
This edition copyright © Dernier Publishing 2018

Published by Dernier Publishing
P.O. Box 793, Orpington, BR6 1FA, England
www.dernierpublishing.com

ISBN: 978-1-912457-17-5

Gillingham and Sittingbourne are real towns in Kent, but the village of Millhurst and the
schools Jess and Brendan attend are completely fictitious.
All characters appearing in this work are fictitious. Any resemblance to real persons, living
or dead, is purely coincidental.

For my wife, Jane

Acknowledgements

I would like to thank Jim Manley, Ruth Millard and Thomas Howlett for their helpful advice, Paul Wintle for reading and commenting on the manuscript, and all of those who have encouraged me, especially Jane, my wife. Above all, I am very grateful to the publisher, Janet Wilson, for all her wisdom and guidance.

Contents

one

Missing Bag

I ran home from school and slammed the front door behind me. Some of our neighbours owned their homes but we rented ours, in the middle of an old estate. It wasn't the poshest part of Gillingham – understatement. Loads of gardens were just junk yards.

A sodden mattress had lain in next door's front garden for weeks, turning black with mould. Rows of garages stood behind the houses. Half of them had their locks smashed, and were decorated with graffiti, which at least added colour to the peeling white paint. Still, it was home.

"Jess," Mum shouted at me from the living room, "the glass in that door is cracked already! You'll have it falling out, slamming it like that. Who's going to pay to get it mended?"

The crack was Dad's doing. He'd chucked a brick at it after Mum threw him out last month. Again.

I didn't answer her. I was already scavenging in the fridge, pulling out half a cucumber, and a plastic box containing left-over potatoes and carrots from Sunday dinner, to see what was at the back. "Mum, there's no orange juice!"

"I know, and I'm not buying any more till next week. There's plenty of water in the tap."

I grabbed a mug from the draining board, filled it at the sink, and carried it to the living room. Mum was working through a basket of ironing. She was dressed in her usual boring jogging pants and T-shirt, hadn't bothered with makeup, and frankly could have done with a decent hair cut, though I didn't say so. She kind of smiled, but not really. "How was your day?"

I pulled off my shoes without untying the laces and slumped into one of the fraying armchairs. "Mrs Gilbert gave me 37% for my history assignment, and I'd spent ages on it. She said it didn't show much evidence of original thought. Said it gave the impression I'd rushed it. And I'd spent three hours doing that last week! Plus, at lunch break I couldn't find my bag, and it's got my maths and French books in it."

"Did you look for it?" Mum asked.

"Everywhere! There's no sign of it. Somebody's either nicked it, or hidden it, just to be nasty."

Mum sighed. "Not again! You should tell Mr Howard."

"I already did. He's useless. I bet it's Alice Davies and her gang. I challenged her, but she just laughed at me."

Mum looked up. "She's not still bullying you, is she?"

"She and her mates have quit punching me when no one's looking. But she still keeps making comments, insinuating that I'm thick, or telling everyone that Dad's in trouble with the police."

"You're not thick, and your dad isn't in trouble with the police – as far as I know." Mum pursed her lips as she folded one of my school shirts and placed it on a pile of clothes on the other armchair. "He's got plenty of faults, and I'm relieved he's not living with us any more, but he's not a criminal."

"Alice annoys me because her mum's always buying her new gear, and I have to make do with the same old clothes, or stuff from charity shops. Her mum always looks smart, too, like she's just stepped off a cat-walk."

"And your mum looks like a rain-soaked cat, I suppose?"

"I didn't mean that, Mum, but neither of us have the money to walk into real shops and buy whatever we like, do we?"

"I'm sorry I can't always be getting you and Brendan the same as other kids, but at least we haven't got a house full of strife, which is the case for lots of the people who live round here." Steam spat from the iron as Mum slammed it down.

"No strife now," I said, "but we had plenty the last time Dad was staying." Mum had let him back again on condition he didn't drink. It only lasted three days. The third day he went out after dinner and came home late. I expect he'd been down the pub. Mum sent Brendan and me upstairs, but we could hear all the shouting. Then there was the sound of broken glass – I found out next morning that was the telly. Then there was more shouting. Finally, the front door slammed, and seconds later came the sound of the brick hitting the glass. "So when are you going to get the front door repaired?"

"When I've got some spare cash. I already owe money to the cash lenders, and I don't want to take out another loan this month. And, by the way, I've told your dad I'm not having him back. We've done it too many times, and it doesn't work. So that's it now."

I stared at her. "So we'll just carry on with no

4

money, and make do without anything new, ever?" I asked. It might have sounded selfish, but honestly, it wasn't new stuff I really cared about. Why couldn't we just be a normal family? Mum shrugged her shoulders, but I could see she was upset, too, so I changed the subject and decided not to think about Dad. "Are there any crisps left?"

"No, and I shan't be getting any unless they're on special offer. Anyway, you'll be having your dinner soon."

"Maybe I should get a paper round, now I'm thirteen. Then I could keep my own personal supply of crisps and fruit juice in my bedroom."

"I'm not sure I fancy you being out in the streets on your own in the early morning. Anyway, what are we going to do about your bag?"

"Mr Howard said that unless I could prove someone had stolen it, there's not much he could do. He said sometimes things turn up in the lost property room."

"Well, I can't afford to buy you another one. There's a bag in the wardrobe in my bedroom that your dad used to take to the gym. You can have that."

"What's for tea, Mum?"

"Fish and chips."

"From the chippy?" I asked, hopefully.

"No, they're too expensive – out of the freezer."

"As usual! Where's Brendan, anyway?"

"Dexter's mum collected them both from school." Brendan's my nine-year-old brother. The two loves of his life are football and food — especially food. He eats and eats, but never seems to get any fatter. "Dexter invited Brendan to play football with him," Mum continued. "Sophie's bringing him back in the car after they've eaten."

"I wish we had a car."

"So do I, but you know full well why we haven't."

"I know, I know, no money, boooring!" I said. "It would be nice to be rich, even if it was only for a week."

"Well, we're not rich, and in fact..." my mother stopped herself.

"In fact, what?" I asked.

"I wasn't going to say it, but you might as well know."

I sat up. "Know what?"

"I tried to draw out some money at the cash machine last week, and discovered we were overdrawn. I rang up the bank, and found out that your dad had withdrawn all the money from our savings account as well, about two months ago."

I stared. "So does that mean we've got nothing?"

"Now that your dad's left, I'm having to claim as a single parent, but it always seems to take the benefits people ages to sort it out."

"So we'll be OK eventually?"

"There's another problem. The landlord wants us out. I got a letter."

Now I was really shocked. "The man who owns our house? But we haven't got anywhere else to go! He can't get rid of us!" I felt a panic coming over me.

"He can. We're behind on the rent. I thought your dad had been paying it, but he must have spent the money on drink. Now the landlord says the rent hasn't been paid for months. He's said he wants us to move out in two months, if we can't pay up. It's all in the letter."

I stared at Mum. "Surely we can do something? What about the council?"

"I think he's within his rights," she said.

"What if we refuse to move?" I said.

"He can get an eviction order from the courts."

"Where will we go?" I asked anxiously.

"We'll have to apply for emergency housing." Mum ironed her duvet cover like it was the landlord, or my dad.

"Emergency housing? What does that mean?"

7

"It might mean the council put us in bed and breakfast accommodation, until they find something else."

"But I won't go. I want to stay here!" I said, getting up and stamping my foot. "This is my home! And Brendan's. And yours!"

"We may have no choice," Mum said with a grimace.

"All because Dad wasted the money! This is the worst day of my life!"

I burst into tears, ran upstairs and threw myself on my bed. Why did everything have to be so awful? I reached for my teddy bear. Rodney's always been there for me, since I was a baby. I clutched Rodney to my chest, and sobbed into my pillow.

two

Sophie's Invitation

"Jess, are you coming down? This is the third time I've called you! Our dinner is getting cold. If you're not here in one minute flat, I'm starting without you."

Mum's voice had finally woken me up. I sat up. I felt ten times worse now than before I slept. I shuffled across the room, and clomped down the stairs.

"What happened to you?" Mum asked.

"I fell asleep," I muttered, sitting at the table. I picked up my fork, and started poking at my fish.

"I thought you were hungry."

"I am; I'm just tired. Wandering all over the school on a Friday afternoon, looking for that bag, has worn me out." I picked up my knife, and started eating.

"Sorry about all the bad news, Jess," said Mum. I didn't reply, but I caught her eye. She was trying to smile. "We'll be all right, we'll sort something out," she promised. "And I'll make sure you see your dad sometimes, if you want to," she added.

I nodded, but didn't want to think about Dad. I wanted to talk about the house, though. "There must be some way we can get enough money to pay the rent, Mum. Couldn't you work more hours at the supermarket now Brendan's getting older?"

"I've tried, but there are no more shifts up for grabs at the moment that fit in with school hours, and I'm not having Brendan home on his own."

"Couldn't you train to do something else, get a proper career – like a nurse or something?"

"I left school with four GCSEs. I don't think they would get me very far. These days you have to go to university and get a degree if you want to be a nurse. That would mean me doing A-levels at the Adult Education Centre first," Mum said.

"But I know you could do it, Mum. Isobel's mum is doing an Open University degree."

"Who's going to pay the bills while I study? When I was sixteen I wanted to do business studies at college, but my dad wasn't having it. He said I had to leave school as soon as I could, and start earning."

"I didn't know you wanted to go into business."

"Well, there you go."

"So what was your first job?" I asked.

"Assistant in a furniture shop. I quite liked it, actually."

"Did you never train as anything, then?"

"No, my geography teacher spoke to me two weeks before I left school. Miss Pearce she was called; I really liked her. She used to treat us like adults, and never raised her voice. She told me that her sister had a hairdressing salon in Rochester, and was looking for a school leaver to train up."

"Did you go for it?"

"I'd have loved to – Dad again. He said I wouldn't earn enough while I was training."

"All I can remember of Grandad," I said, "is him sitting in his lounge, smoking. Oh, and he had a big cage full of green and blue budgies out in the garden."

"He wasn't unkind," Mum said, "but he was short-sighted when it came to my future. I know I could have made a success of being a hairdresser. I would probably have had my own business in time. I used to dream about running my own salon." She paused. "Now look at me! Anyway I fell pregnant with you, and I had so much sickness, I had to give up work. Now it's just history."

"But you could do something now," I said.

That moment the door bell rang. It was Dexter's mum arriving with Brendan. She was younger than Mum, and sounded a bit posh.

"Hi, Sophie!" Mum said. "Thanks for having Brendan."

"No problem, they've had fun, but I'm sorry, Tracy, Brendan grazed his knee badly playing football. I cleaned it up, but he was limping a bit, so the boys' game was cut short."

"No worries; he'll live," Mum said, taking a look at the damage. "Does it hurt, Brendan?"

"It's a bit sore," Brendan said, "and the antiseptic stuff stung, but it's much better now."

"Perhaps you should spend a night in Medway Hospital," I said mockingly, "as it's such a big scratch!"

"Jess!" Mum said. "That's not a nice thing for a sister to say. You wouldn't have liked it if it had been the other way round."

I shoved his arm and grinned at him and he grinned back. He knew I didn't mean it. "We went out to Burger King!" Brendan told me as he pushed past. He talks just like Dad when he's excited.

"Lucky you!" I said. "We had fish out of the freezer."

Brendan dropped his football boots on the floor, and went upstairs to play on his Playstation, clomping more than usual due to his wounded knee.

He reminded me of Dad again, the way he walked up the stairs.

"Do you want to come in?" Mum asked Sophie.

"Thanks Tracy, but I'd better be getting back. Just a thought though, Brendan gets on so well with Dexter that Keiran and I have had an idea. We've booked a cottage in Devon for the first week of the school holidays. What do you think about our taking Brendan with us?"

My eyes opened wide. A holiday in a cottage in Devon! Lucky Brendan! I wished I could have a holiday in a cottage or a caravan, or even go camping like my friend Isobel.

"I'm sure he'd love it," Mum said with a proper smile – the first I'd seen all day. "There's no way I can afford to take the kids away for a holiday this year."

"I'm sorry, Tracy," Sophie said with a kind smile. "I know money's tight for you."

"You can say that again," Mum said with a sigh.

"Life has its ups and downs, doesn't it? Keiran's business is doing very well at the moment. Suddenly a lot of people seem to want new kitchens, so he's got lots of orders and we thought we'd have a little break – it was a bit cheaper as it was last minute."

"That's great, Sophie," Mum said. "You both work hard, you deserve it."

"Maybe it will be your turn for something good next," Sophie said, squeezing Mum's arm. "I hope something will turn up for you soon."

"Well I'm pretty sure the next few days will see a few envelopes turning up on my doormat, reminding me someone would like paying."

Sophie leaned towards Mum. I don't think she wanted me to hear, but I heard anyway. "All I can say is, if things do get really desperate, please let me know. Now, I must be off. Keiran wants to go out to the gym, so I need to get back with the car."

I looked at Mum. She had tears in her eyes, just like me.

three

Sports Day

"Mum, have you seen my white shorts? I've looked everywhere for them," I called. I was standing at the top of the stairs.

It was Sports Day at our school – probably the best day of the year for me. All my problems disappear for the afternoon; I simply get caught up in the excitement of running. Brendan's thing is football – mine is running. Dad always liked sport. We take after him, not that that was top of my mind right then.

"They're in the second drawer from the top, where they're supposed to be. I washed them on Saturday. Your running vest is there as well," Mum said.

"Found them!" I called from my bedroom. Ten seconds later, the door bell rang.

"Jess! Isobel's here," Mum shouted up the stairs. Isobel's my best friend. We've been in the same class since we started school. She's got jet-black hair and dark eyes, with perfect eyebrows and long lashes. I think she had an Indian great-grandmother, but what I like most about her is that she's always smiling. When you have a family like mine, it helps.

I ran down the stairs. "Hi Isobel, I'm ready. Bye, Mum. See you later! And keep your fingers crossed that the rain stops," I called back, as I ran out of the front door.

"Good luck," she called after me. "It's only a bit of drizzle, it'll be fine."

I slammed the door behind me, forgetting about the cracked glass again. Luckily it didn't fall out. Isobel giggled and I grinned back. Today, nothing mattered, only running.

As Mum had predicted, the drizzle didn't last long, and by lunchtime blue sky was appearing in the grey cloud over the school sports ground. I was one of the first out there, loosening up on the grass in the warm-up area. I'm tall for my age – like Brendan. It's something I've inherited from Dad.

I tried not to think about Dad, though, as I concentrated on stretching and warming up ready for the race, and getting my head in gear. My best distance is the 300 metres, but Miss Bates, the PE teacher, said she thought that I could pull off the 200 metres as well, so she'd put me in for both races. Miss

Bates is short and stocky, and looks like she should have been a sergeant major. When she gets annoyed she shouts like one, too!

I was hoping I could at least beat Alice Davies' best mate and number two bully, Nicola Winter, in the 200 metres, even if I didn't come first. Isobel was in the race, too.

And so Sports Day began. It started with the high jump and long jump events, then the runners were lining up for the older boys' 100 metres. Then it was our turn.

"All girls for the 200 metres, present at the starting-line," the marshal's voice crackled over the public address system. I was the tallest in the line-up. Isobel and I high-fived – she knew I would beat her, but she smiled anyway. I didn't look at Nicola, but I knew she was there, two lanes away to my right.

Sunshine broke through the clouds as we got into position. Miss Bates raised her arm, fired the starting pistol, and we were off. I made a good start, and as we came off the bend into the straight, I started to pull ahead of the other girls. I was aware of Isobel, a couple of metres behind me, and I assumed Nicola must have been further behind.

I tried to increase my speed. Suddenly I was conscious of Nicola coming up on my right. I was straining to keep ahead of her. In the final ten metres she slid past me. Now she was half a length in front, and I just couldn't catch her up. We reached the tape, and Nicola went through first!

I stood near the finishing line, holding my sides, recovering my breath. My heart was pounding in my chest. Isobel came up and put her arms around me.

"You were brilliant!" she said breathlessly.

"Not brilliant enough," I gasped. I was angry that Nicola had beaten me. I should have increased my speed a few metres earlier.

Isobel and I walked slowly over to where our year was hanging out. "Beaten by Nicola," I groaned. "Of all people!"

Isobel gave me a hug. "Don't let her get to you."

We sat on the grass getting our breath back. The public address system sounded again. "Winner of the girls 200 metres: Nicola Winter, 27.5 seconds; second, Jessica Hargreaves, 27.7 seconds; third, Grace Hughes, 28.1 seconds."

27.7 seconds was a personal best!

four

Racing Ahead

Beating my personal best ever time was a small consolation prize. "If only it'd been someone other than Nicola who came first," I complained to Isobel. I glanced to the left, only to see Alice and Nicola exchanging remarks and sniggering in my direction. "Don't look at them, Isobel," I said. "Pretend you haven't noticed."

"That's what I keep telling you, Jess," she said. "Just ignore them."

"How is it they always manage to get one up on me?" I groaned.

"Forget about them, Jess. You're better off without them." After a short silence she added, "Your Dad's not been back then?"

"No," I said. "According to Mum, he's never coming back. You don't know how lucky you are to

19

have parents who get on."

"I wish there was something I could do to help you."

"Just being my friend helps," I said with a sigh. "I wish we could go back to how it used to be at home, seems like ages ago now, doing things as a family; holidays, movies and stuff."

The loudspeaker interrupted our conversation. "Competitors for the girls 300 metres, report to the starting marshal."

"That's me," I said, jumping up.

"Best of luck," Isobel said. "You can do it, Jess. I'll be rooting for you."

After another quick warm-up I was on the starting line again. Nicola was in this race too, but I knew I could beat her at this distance. The danger came from Samantha Sanderson, and Aasha Gill. I knew I mustn't rush the first hundred metres. As long as they didn't get too far ahead for me to catch up with them. . . I went over the race in my mind, keeping up with the rest, then overtaking.

We were on our marks. Miss Bates held up the pistol again and fired. Two seconds later, the pistol sounded a second time. False start! Samantha had moved too soon. We lined up once more. The pistol cracked again, and this time it was a good start. Aasha took the lead and was striding ahead, with Samantha in second place. In the back straight we were all close together, except for Aasha who was well in front. I began to inch past the others, and Samantha put on the pressure at the same time. We were both closing in on Aasha as we went round the bend.

With one hundred metres to go, Samantha was only two metres behind her, but I was close on Samantha's heels. Aasha increased her speed, but so did Samantha and I. Now we were in the final fifty metres, and Samantha edged past Aasha. I thought my chest was going to burst. Aasha was slipping back, and the tape was in front. The crowd was roaring.

I strained with all my might, willing my legs to stretch a bit further. I drew neck and neck with Samantha. We seemed to hit the tape simultaneously.

I collapsed on the grass, and rolled onto my back looking up at the small clouds racing across the blue sky. I was hot, breathless and exhausted; my legs were killing me. Isobel ran over and pulled me to my feet.

"Jess, you were awesome!" she said, giving me a hug.

We walked, arm in arm, to our section of the sports field. This time it was my turn to smirk in Alice's direction, but she avoided eye contact. Other friends in my year started to congratulate me, but I was listening for the scores.

"We'll have to wait for the result," I said. "It was so close!"

Waiting for the announcement seemed to take forever. At last the speaker system sputtered into action. "The result of the girls 300 hundred metres: in first place, Jessica Hargreaves: 44.9 seconds; second, Samantha Sanderson: 45.0 seconds; third, Aasha Gill: 45.3 seconds."

"You've won! You've won," Isobel shouted. She couldn't stop jumping up and down.

I looked behind as I joined her. Alice and Nicola were walking away.

five

Encounter in Town

The next Saturday I had to go to the library. Brendan and Dexter had been playing a stupid computer game on the laptop after school the day before. Outcome? They'd succeeded in crashing it. So I couldn't do my English literature assignment on it. Great!

Mum had no cash, so we couldn't get the laptop fixed, which is why I had to get the bus to town, to use one of the computers at the public library. Fortunately I still had my library card, even though I hadn't used it for almost a year.

There were two computer stations free. I was given one sandwiched between a man who looked like he was doing some kind of job application, and an old woman with purple hair. She was watching a YouTube clip of some concert from the sixties, by the look of the clothes. Fortunately for me she had headphones, but that didn't stop her swaying from side to side, presumably to the music. How can people do that in a public place? So embarrassing.

In my allotted hour I managed to stitch together a fairly presentable piece on *Call of the Wild*, a book about a sled dog in the Canadian forests, who gets beaten and badly treated, but learns how to survive in a harsh environment. It was a pretty tough life being a sled dog, by the sound of it; they got bullied, too. Still, he overcame his issues and later he became the leader of his team. In my conclusion I wrote that maybe one day I would overcome my issues and succeed, too. Teachers like that sort of thing.

I had twenty minutes to spare before the next bus back, and debated about going to McDonald's for a milkshake, but decided it was a waste of money doing that on my own, so I wandered down the High Street looking in the windows. As I passed the newsagent, a man in a checked shirt was coming out. I'd have passed him if he hadn't called out. "Jess!" he said.

I turned and got a shock. It was Dad! "Dad!" I said. "What are you doing here?"

"I was looking at the photography magazines," he said. "Can't afford to buy anything, of course." Dad used to have a good camera and loved doing photography. He used to take pictures of Brendan and me on birthdays and holidays and stuff. That was before the alcohol took over. He probably sold the camera to buy drink. If he hadn't spoken, I would never have recognised him, because he looked like he hadn't shaved for a week. "It's great seeing you, Jess," he said.

Seeing him was such a shock I blurted out the first thing that came to my mind. "Are you growing a beard or can't you afford razors, either?"

"Bit of both, I guess. I've never had a beard so I wondered what it would look like."

"I prefer the original version."

"Jess, it's good seeing you again," he repeated, a bit more quietly this time.

"Yeah, well..." I couldn't bring myself to say I was pleased to see him too, cos I wasn't sure that I was. I didn't want to lie, but the truth was harsh. Anyway, I think he guessed.

"I don't blame you for not wanting to see me."

I shrugged. "You've left us on our own, with no money."

"You don't have to rub it in," Dad said quietly, looking down. "I feel guilty enough as it is."

"Where are you living now?" I asked. "Mum said you're in some kind of institution."

"It's a men's hostel in Rochester," he said. "It's pretty basic, but at least I have my own room and a bed."

"I suppose I should be thankful my dad isn't sleeping in a shop doorway. And at least none of my schoolmates is in sight watching me talk to you."

He sighed. "You must hate me for what I've done."

I had to pause and think about that one, as we stood on the pavement, looking at each other like strangers. "I don't hate you, Dad. You're still my dad." I looked at him, standing there looking like a tramp. "But I hate the alcohol. And what it's done to you." His face was thin and haggard. Suddenly I felt sorry for him. He'd always tried to do his best for Brendan and me in the past, before he'd started drinking too much. We were in people's way on the pavement and they were giving us dirty looks as they passed, but I ignored them. So did Dad.

"Not a father to be proud of, am I, Jess?"

"I wish we could go back to the way it was before." I swallowed hard. "Mum does her best, but it's not the same without you there."

He hung his head. "But it's peaceful, now," he said.

I nodded. "I got scared when you and Mum were arguing. And you broke the telly, and the glass in the door."

"You're better off without me," he said, and turned his face away, but I could see tears in his eyes. Despite everything, a lump came to my throat.

"Dad, is anyone helping you to stop drinking?"

"Yes, I go to a group. Actually, I haven't had a drink for three weeks now." I looked at him again. Despite everything, I did miss him. I reached up and gave him a quick hug. "I've got to run now," I said, checking my watch, "or I'll miss my bus."

"OK, Jess," Dad said. "Thanks for stopping to talk to me. I'll see you sometime."

I turned quickly and hurried back to the bus stop. This time it was me that was welling up.

I held it together while I was on the bus, but my thoughts were going round and round. If only we could turn the clock back to how it used to be! If only Dad would stop drinking!

six

The Letter

I didn't tell Mum about meeting Dad. When I got in, I went straight upstairs and had a bit of a cry in my room. I couldn't get Dad out of my mind. Stupid Dad! Stupid alcohol!

After a while I washed my face and went down to the kitchen. After helping myself to a handful of chocolate chip cookies from an open packet, I called out to mum who was in the living room. "Do you want a cup of tea?"

"That would be nice, thanks."

"What are you doing?" I asked, raising my voice above the noise of the washing machine that had just gone into its spin cycle.

"Reading a letter," Mum answered.

"Anything interesting?"

"As a matter of fact, yes," she answered, coming into the kitchen. "It's a letter from my Auntie Joan."

"Is she the one who always puts a letter in with her Christmas card?"

"Yes, she's your great-aunt, your grandad's sister. I haven't seen her since his funeral. You were only about six then, so you didn't go. I send her a letter every Christmas, too, so she knows all about us."

"She must be pretty old," I said.

"She was older than my dad," Mum said, "so she must be in her seventies."

"Why has she written to you when it's not Christmas?" I asked. "She hasn't sent us loads of money, has she?"

"No, but it might be something even better than that."

At this I became interested. "What's better than money?"

"A new life," Mum replied.

"Are you in philosophical mode today or something?" I asked. "If so, you could do my history assignment."

The washing machine reached the end of its cycle, so we could now talk without shouting. "I'll read the letter out to you," she said, "because it concerns you as much as me."

I wondered what on earth it could have to do with me.

Mum sat down at the table, and spread out the letter, cup of tea forgotten. I leaned over her shoulder.

"Her handwriting's rather scrawly," Mum said, "so it's hard to read, but I think I've worked most of it out. And just to warn you, I told her your dad had left before Christmas. She doesn't know he's been back since."

I raised my eyebrows but didn't reply. She read out the letter slowly:

Dear Tracy,

You will be surprised to receive a letter from me. I've put off writing for several weeks, but after a lot of thought, I have a proposition to make. I'm not as strong as I used to be, as you can probably guess from my writing. I'm not up to much physical work these days. My neighbours keep telling me I should be employing somebody to look after the house; cleaning, polishing, laundry and so on. I already pay a man to look after the garden, and chop up the logs for firewood, but I don't fancy having a stranger coming into the house and going through all my things.

So I've been trying to think whom I could have to help me. I've decided I'd rather have someone in the family to give me a hand, but, of course, none of you live in the village any more. Not that you ever did, of course. Your father left Millhurst many years ago, when he got an apprenticeship in Chatham Dockyard.

That's why I'm writing to you now. You've always struck me as sensible and kind. You are still young and strong, and this is a big house. There's enough room here for you and Jess and Brendan. I know coming here would be a big upheaval for you, and the children would have to change schools, but Millhurst is a lovely village, and I'm sure they would make new friends. I wouldn't ask you to pay anything for lodgings or food.

I worked in the bank most of my working life, so I have a good pension. I'd be willing to pay you an allowance for keeping the house. We can discuss that and agree on a figure, if you're at all interested.

Please give this serious thought. I'm not expecting you to decide immediately, but when you are ready I want you to come over here and we can talk it all through. I will pay for a taxi – and please bring your children, I would like to meet them.

Please note, I didn't say inspect them. I may be old, but I don't think I'm a strict old fusspot!

I've written my telephone number at the top of the letter, so give me a call when you are ready.

With my love,

Joan

My jaw had dropped open. "Where's Millhurst?" I asked.

"Just outside Sittingbourne," Mum said. "It's a little village in the countryside; your Grandad and Granny used to take me to visit her when I was small."

"We're not going to live in the countryside, are we?" I asked, with a frown. One minute Mum tells me we are being forced out of our home; now she's telling me we may be quitting Gillingham altogether!

"That's what we need to decide. Like Auntie Joan said, we don't have to rush into a decision."

"I'm not leaving Gillingham, and all my friends."

Mum tapped on the table with her fingernails. "Well, you'd be leaving Alice Davies behind, and it's near enough that you and your friends could still visit each another."

I folded my arms. "I'm not going!"

"We all need to think about it. It's a big decision. You know how short of money we are."

"Don't I just? Isobel's off to Canterbury shopping today, and I haven't even got the money to go to the cinema."

"Exactly. I don't know how much Auntie Joan would pay me, but with free food and lodgings we certainly couldn't be worse off."

"I bet the schools are rubbish round there," I said, raising my voice.

Mum stared back. "How do you know that?"

"I don't want to move," I said. I took two mugs off the draining board and slammed them on the table.

"We haven't told Brendan yet," Mum said. "He needs to be in on the decision as well."

I made the tea in silence and stomped upstairs with mine. Who did this interfering Auntie Joan think she was, suggesting we all uproot, just because she couldn't manage to look after herself any more?

I slumped on my bed, and pulled Rodney off his chair.

"They're trying to get us to move, Rodney. Dad's living in a hostel; our family's broken up. Now between the landlord and this stupid old Auntie Joan, they're trying to throw us out of this house. Why can't everyone just leave us alone?"

seven

The Old Aunt

Brendan was the first to jump out of the taxi. It had only taken us thirty minutes to get from Gillingham to Millhurst.

I have to admit, in the week between getting the letter and going to Auntie Joan's, I had started to have second thoughts about the move. Alice Davies and her friends had been as nasty as ever. I found my old school bag, right at the bottom of the lost property box. No way did it get there by accident. And not until after I'd got into trouble for not having my French book in class.

I didn't tell Mum, but I'd checked out Millhurst when I was round Isobel's, on her tablet. There was a village website: it *looked* a million miles from Gillingham, with its ancient church and old-fashioned buildings and proper cottage gardens, but actually it wasn't that far. Isobel and me had discussed it, and I promised to have a bit more of an open mind about it, because how much worse could it be than going into temporary accommodation?

We'd agreed, though, that I would say no if there wasn't enough room for her to come and stay, or if Auntie Joan was grim, which frankly we were expecting. I mean, who'd want to live with a dinosaur aunt you didn't even know?

In the morning sunshine the village looked pretty enough to be one of the pictures on jigsaw puzzle boxes you see on the bottom shelf in charity shops.

The village high street was mostly made up of ancient red-brick cottages and at the end there was a historical-looking pub; white with black wooden beams. All down the main road there were tubs brimming with red geraniums. It was like people cared about where they lived, not like round our way. Opposite the pub was a massive grey stone church, with a square tower.

The taxi driver turned into a narrow lane, and there at the end, surrounded by trees, was Auntie Joan's cottage.

Mum had put on her best outfit – a scarlet, short-sleeved dress, with matching shoes. Actually, she looked good in it. First time she'd bothered with her appearance for ages, so if nothing else good came of the trip, at least there was that.

Auntie Joan had invited us to stay from Saturday morning to Sunday afternoon, which seemed way too long to me. What a waste of a weekend! Auntie Joan had said to Mum on the phone that it would give us more time to get to know one another. Really? I told Mum one hour might be long enough for me to confirm that I wanted to stay in Gillingham. I thought Brendan would be on my side, but even though Mum hadn't told him about the landlord wanting us out, he had already decided that if the garden was big enough for him to play football in, he wanted to stay for ever, and packed his football boots just in case.

Mum hadn't been trying to pressurise me into accepting the move, but I sensed that she really wanted it to work out. She was nervous, though. She asked me what she should wear and after she'd tried on her dress she looked so cheerful I didn't want to burst her bubble. Time enough for that later. Maybe she'd hate it, too, then I wouldn't have to do any persuading.

But I wasn't making any promises.

So, anyway, there we were, getting out of the taxi in front of Auntie Joan's cottage. "Cottage" seemed a funny name for what was really a large old house, standing in its own grounds. The lower part of the house was made of brick, painted white. In the middle was a black, heavy wooden front door, with windows on either side. The top half of the house was clad in red tiles, pierced by two lattice windows. The roof sloped up to a tall brick chimney.

"Wow!" said Brendan, his eyes lighting up when he saw the size of the house, and the massive garden, going round both sides. He asked to borrow my mobile phone to take some photos. "I want to show this to Dexter. He'll be amazed that this is where we're coming to live."

"Correction," I said, snatching my phone back. "Where we *may* be coming to live. Nothing has been decided yet. Remember?" If Brendan thought he was going to steam-roller me into moving house, he was wrong. It might look like a fabulous holiday place, but there were other considerations if you were going to *live* somewhere.

Auntie Joan must have heard the taxi pulling up cos she was standing at the door, wearing a smart navy skirt and cream blouse. It made her look elegant, not a bit like the doddery old lady I'd expected, which was a nice surprise, cos she'd sounded ancient in her letter. Appearances can be deceiving, though, I warned myself. She might have a whole list of rules we'd have to follow.

I let Brendan and my mother walk up the gravel

path in front of me. Auntie Joan was beaming at us all. "Tracy, how lovely to see you," she said. "I wouldn't have recognised you. That colour suits you."

"It's the only dress she's got that fits," Brendan said.

"Brendan!" Mum said, looking at him reproachfully. *Trust him to put his foot in it*, I thought, giving him a shove from behind.

"It's been so many years since we've seen each other," said Auntie Joan, pretending not to hear. "I got out my photograph album yesterday. Your father sent me a picture of Jess when she was a new-born; he was so proud to be a grandfather. Now look how you have grown up, Jess! That makes me feel old."

So it should, I thought, but I forced myself to smile.

"But why am I keeping you all here on the doorstep?" Auntie Joan said. "Go along in, and find a soft chair while I pay the taxi driver." She bent down to kiss my brother's cheek. "Hello, Brendan, come along in," she said. He grimaced, and wiped his cheek with his sleeve.

It was my turn next. I suffered the kiss, then the three of us stepped through the front door straight into the living room. It was like walking into a museum. *We must be in some kind of time warp*, I thought. I'd visited a local museum with school, not long before. In the Victorian section was a reconstructed 19th-century street with old-fashioned shops and houses. This living room would have fitted in perfectly.

The sofas and armchairs were flowery, as was the carpet and the wallpaper. There was way too much dark furniture, in my opinion, and all of it covered with artefacts. There were even ornaments attached to the beams on the ceiling. In the centre of the room was a coffee table with cups and saucers set out, and a plate, but you couldn't see what was on it, because it was covered with a white lacy cloth.

At least the chairs were arranged around a decent-sized TV. It was probably the only thing in the room that wasn't antique.

Mum sat herself down in one of the armchairs. Then turning to Brendan and me, she said, "You two can share the sofa. And behave, the pair of you."

"She doesn't look very rich," Brendan said.

"Shh! She might hear you," Mum told him.

"This furniture looks like it came out of a museum," I said in a half whisper. "If we have to move, can we bring our own?"

"Well none of ours is much good," Mum said. "There won't be room for two lots of furniture here."

We fell silent as Auntie Joan came back into the room. "I've asked the taxi driver to call back for you at four o'clock tomorrow afternoon. Will that be all right for you?"

"That'll be fine, thank you," Mum replied.

Auntie Joan smiled back. "Good, you've all made yourselves comfortable. Now, first we'll have a little morning snack, and then I expect you'll want to explore the cottage. Do you all drink tea?"

"I don't like tea," Brendan said, pulling a face.

"Do you have any juice, please, Auntie Joan?" I asked, thinking one of us ought to appear more obliging.

"I have some squash. There's orange, or lemon and barley water."

"Orange, please," I said. You'd have to be ancient to like lemon and barley water, I thought.

"And me," said Brendan.

"Please!" Mum added, giving him a stern look.

"I'll just put the kettle on then," said Auntie Joan.

She returned a few minutes later carrying a tray with a teapot covered in a pink and white tea-cosy, a china milk jug and two glasses of squash. "Tracy, will you be mother, and pour out the tea, please? Now, that's a silly thing to say; you are Jess and Brendan's mother!"

Mum poured the milk and tea into two blue and white china cups that matched the jug and teapot. "I bought some Viennese slices yesterday," said Auntie

Joan, taking the cloth off the plate. "If you children prefer, I've also got some chocolate marshmallows."

"They're my favourite!" said Brendan, his face lighting up.

"That's good," Auntie Joan said, offering the plate to Brendan. "And what about you, Jess?" she asked, turning to me with a smile.

"I'll have a marshmallow, too, please," I replied, trying not to grit my teeth at being lumped as "children" with Brendan.

"You must finish them up before you go," said Auntie Joan, settling back into the remaining armchair. "Right, now that we're all set up, I want you to tell me all about yourselves. Not your secrets; we're all allowed to keep those. I want to know what you like to do, and what you don't like. Let's start with Mum; go on Tracy."

This was beginning to sound like an inquisition. I was glad I wasn't the first to be interrogated.

eight

The Interrogation

"I don't know where to begin," said Mum, quickly trying to gather her thoughts. "I've told you about Trevor and me," she started.

"Well," said Auntie Joan, "I know that you're no longer living together, and from your letters I understand there was a lot of friction between the two of you the last year or two."

"Friction! You could say that again. When Trevor had been drinking he could lose his temper and sometimes smashed things."

"Oh, dear, I didn't realise it was that bad," said Auntie Joan. "Has he moved right away?"

"No, he's living in a hostel in Rochester."

"He's growing a beard now," I said. As soon as the words were out of my mouth I realised I should have kept my mouth shut.

"How do you know that, Jess?" asked Mum, looking alarmed.

"I bumped into him when I went to the library last Saturday," I said, feeling my cheeks colour up.

"Jess, you never told me that," Mum said. "Why didn't you tell me before?"

"I thought it would upset you," I replied.

"He hadn't contacted you?"

"No, it was just coincidence. He was coming out of a shop as I was waiting for the bus." Mum's face had gone red, too. I could see this wasn't at all the good impression she'd been hoping to make with Auntie Joan and I felt a bit bad.

"I must apologise, Auntie Joan," Mum said. "We shouldn't be having a row in front of you. It's just that... it's just that Trevor has hurt me so very much. Perhaps I shouldn't feel so bitter towards him, but I do."

"Tracy, I haven't been through the things you've experienced," Auntie Joan said, "but I can understand your feelings. And as for having a tiff in front of me: if you all decide it's right for you to move here, we're going to have to get used to seeing what each of us is really like."

"Mum," I said, "I'm sorry I didn't tell you about meeting Dad."

"Maybe it would have been better if you'd told me sooner, Jess," Mum said.

"I was afraid you'd be hurt whenever I said it."

"You're probably right, but I don't like to think you're keeping things from me."

I was feeling in a bit of a no-win situation. I hadn't wanted to upset Mum unnecessarily, and I didn't want to be keeping secrets, either. I sighed. If only our family could be together again; if only we could go back to how it used to be!

"But tell me," Auntie Joan said, interrupting my thoughts. "What would you like to do with your life, Tracy? You're still young."

"It doesn't look like a young woman who stares back at me from the mirror each morning," Mum said, recovering her composure.

"You're still young compared to me. How old are you, if I may ask?"

"Thirty-three last month. You asked me what I'd like to do. If I had a fairy godmother I'd ask her to whisk me away to a tropical island, or to the south of France, or Italy, or somewhere like that. And I'd like to be rich. No, not rich; I'd like to succeed at something."

"Don't let go of that dream, dear. Hold on to it, and it may come true," said Auntie Joan. Then there was a bit of a silence while she seemed to be deep in thought. Me and Brendan exchanged a look. His mouth was full of marshmallow but that didn't stop him grinning. I made a face at him.

After a few moments, Auntie Joan turned to me. "Jess, you look like a bright girl. What do you like doing?" There was a warmth in the way she said it which took me by surprise, and I realised she looked a bit like my Mum when she smiled.

"I like sport – especially running, and I like swimming and spending time with my friends."

"That's a wonderful combination. Tell me more about the running," Auntie Joan said. She didn't seem to be putting on a show or making conversation for the sake of it.

"We had our Sports Day recently; I won the 300 metres race, and I came second in the 200 metres. Our house won the school trophy."

"Well done, that's excellent!" she said, with a warm smile. "You must keep going with it. I know you must be anxious about having to move school if you should come to live here. I've been asking my neighbours. They say that two of the schools in Sittingbourne are very good, and one of them has an excellent reputation for sport, so I'm sure you could continue your running."

"I know that," I said. "I checked out the local schools on the internet."

"I didn't know you'd done that, Jess," Mum said.

I quickly changed the subject, before I could be accused of keeping that from her, too. "Are there any young people living in the village?" I asked. "It seems very quiet."

"Yes, quite a few. In fact, I was speaking to the vicar this week, and he told me that the youth group he runs in the church hall has about a dozen members. So although it's not big, you could make some friends there."

"But I'd miss my best friend, Isobel, if we came here."

"Well, look, Jess," said Auntie Joan. "In a minute we'll go up and see the bedrooms. They're not large, but if Isobel doesn't mind sleeping on the floor in your room in a sleeping bag, she's welcome to come and stay just as often as you like."

"Thanks," I said. I was sensing my resistance to moving to Millhurst beginning to break down. Auntie Joan might be old, but perhaps she wasn't so bad after all. It was like she understood how things really were.

"And now, sir," Auntie Joan said, turning to my brother. "What has this young man got to say for himself? What sort of things do you like doing, Brendan?"

"I'm good at football. I'm in the school team," Brendan replied proudly.

"Very good. So both of you like sport. I used to play a lot of tennis, and I used to enjoy swimming, too. I don't know much about football. They hadn't thought of ladies' football in my day, as far as I can remember. I'm sure you'd be able to join a football team if you came to live here, Brendan. The local primary school is bound to have a football team."

"I'm good at drawing and painting, too," he said.

"I'd very much like to see some of your drawings," Auntie Joan said. "I had a younger sister, Sybil; she was a very keen artist. That's one of her paintings behind you – the one of the robin. Sadly she died young, after suffering from a bad chest for years."

"I'd forgotten you and Dad had a younger sister," said Mum, then she added, "Sorry about that."

"That's all right, it was a long time ago now."

There was a bit of an uncomfortable pause, before Brendan asked: "May I have another marshmallow please?"

"Please do. I told you, they're for you and Jess to share. Then I think we should all explore the cottage."

"You haven't told us what you like, Auntie Joan," I said, "apart from tennis and swimming when you were younger." She was beginning to intrigue me. "Did you get married? Have you got any children?"

"No, I never married or had children. I worked in the bank and used to write a lot of short stories in my spare time. I don't do much of that now, but I haven't lost my imagination. I still like to make up stories in my head."

"What kind of stories?" I asked, but Auntie Joan didn't get a chance to reply because at that moment there was a loud crash upstairs.

Brendan jumped up. "You must have a burglar," he said.

nine

The Burglar

"Don't be so dramatic, Brendan!" I said. "There's not going to be a burglar on a Saturday morning!"

"We'd better go and see what's happened, though," Auntie Joan said. "We may as well start the tour upstairs."

We followed her through a door to the hall, and up a narrow staircase. The first room we came to had bare wooden floorboards, except for a red and green rug next to the bed, which was positioned against the centre of the opposite wall. At the foot of the bed was a small table, upon which lay a glass vase containing pink carnations, lying on its side. Water dripped from the top of the table onto the floor. The "burglar" was sitting on the windowsill – a fat ginger cat, swishing his tail, looking oblivious to what he had done.

"Oh, Bernard!" Auntie Joan scolded. "What are

49

you doing in my bedroom? I might have known it was you."

Bernard mewed a greeting, and Auntie Joan picked him up. "Come and see some new friends."

I stroked Bernard on his head and smiled. He looked at me suspiciously. "We had a ginger and white cat once, called Ginger," I said, "Not a very imaginative name, was it? He got run over in our street. It was awful. I wanted another cat, but Mum didn't want to risk another one being killed and, anyway, she said we couldn't afford to feed it."

"If you come here, you can share Bernard," Auntie Joan said. "As you can see by the size of him, he likes his food. He's not used to strangers; otherwise he'd have been downstairs, begging for a share of the cakes."

"I bet he keeps the mice down," Mum said, "Since we lost Ginger we keep seeing mice in our kitchen."

"I haven't seen a mouse for years," Auntie Joan said, "but we sometimes have rats around the outhouse."

"Rats!" cried Brendan. "I shall keep a baseball bat by my bed if we live here."

Mum gave him a sharp look and he shut up.

"Now we're upstairs we might as well see round all the bedrooms," Auntie Joan said, leading us down a corridor. "Tracy, I thought you could have this next one. All the rooms are dry, or at least they were until Bernard knocked over the vase! The lady next door has been helping me to air the bedding. I don't have these modern duvets, I'm afraid – just blankets and eiderdowns."

"We could bring duvets from our house," Mum said, seeing me and Brendan look at each other in horror.

We walked into the second bedroom. There was an ancient bed with a pink quilt. In the corner was a wooden wardrobe. It looked like it was years since anyone had ever slept in this room. Mum noticed a painting of the village church on the wall, and she stood looking at it.

I joined her. "Did your sister paint that one too?" I asked.

"Yes, dear, she did. Do you see that patch of poppies by the beech tree in the churchyard in the picture? That's where she's buried. This used to be Sybil's room. She used to love the view across the fields from here."

"You must miss her a lot," I said.

"I did, but it's a long time ago now. I often remember the things we did together when we were children. There were three of us then. We had to make our own entertainment in those days. Ben, your grandad, used to love to make dens out of branches and ferns in the wood at the bottom of a big field. Sybil and I would collect all the broken saucepans and crockery we could find, and serve up pretend meals. Before she took so poorly, Sybil and I loved to go for walks in the woods, and gather flowers. You are not allowed to pick them these days, of course." It sounded old-fashioned, but fun. I smiled at her and she smiled back. "The best time was in the summer; when they did the hay-making," she continued. "My father cut and baled the hay, and we would stack up the bales. He used to let us pile them up like castles, and other children from the village would come and join us. Then at tea time, father would collect mother on the back of the tractor, and she would come laden with a big bowl of strawberries, a pot of cream and bottles of lemonade."

I could see them doing that here, it was that kind of place. It was another planet from our estate in Gillingham. "What did you do in the winter?" I asked.

"We would have musical evenings," Auntie Joan replied with a soft smile. "Sybil and I both played the piano. Sometimes I would accompany Sybil on the piano whilst she sang a solo. She had a lovely singing voice, much better than mine."

"Which room's mine?" asked Brendan, who was getting bored with all the talking.

"We have to go up another flight of stairs to the

attic," Auntie Joan said. "There's one room up there, and then there's another on the other side of the house. You two are going to have to decide who sleeps where."

Brendan ran up the next narrow flight of stairs and looked in the attic bedroom. "I want this room, Jess!"

"You haven't seen the other one yet," I said, joining him, "and remember, we're only staying *one night*. We haven't decided to move yet."

"I want to be at the top of the house," Brendan said. "And it's you who haven't decided; I think we should move to Millhurst."

I didn't say anything, because Brendan was only half right. I was starting to think this might not be so bad after all, just as Brendan did a giant leap backwards onto the bed. It wobbled and gave a crack.

"You can't just jump around like that, Brendan!" Mum said. "I'm so sorry, Auntie Joan."

Auntie Joan laughed. "Boys will be boys. This was your grandfather's room, a very long time ago. The bedding and curtains are all very faded in here aren't they? We'll have to buy something new."

"I'd still like to have this room," Brendan said. "I could bring my football duvet cover."

"We haven't seen the last bedroom yet, to see whether I like it," I objected. It seemed like I wasn't

53

getting much choice in all of this. I was starting to feel a bit anxious. If I didn't like the last bedroom. . .

"You're quite right, Jess," said Auntie Joan. "We mustn't jump the gun."

"But where is the other room?" I asked.

ten

A Chair for Rodney

"We have to go through this passageway to get to the last bedroom," said Auntie Joan, after we'd gone back down the little flight of stairs, indicating a short landing with a small window that looked out on to the front garden. Brendan pushed past and ran on in front once more.

"Slow down, Brendan, this is not a race!" Mum snapped.

"Hey, there's another set of stairs going down on this side of the house!" he shouted.

"Yes, they don't build many houses like this nowadays," Auntie Joan said. "This cottage was built by my great-grandfather; it's nearly a hundred and fifty years old. He used to own the farm before my grandfather and father, of course."

"Is it haunted?" Brendan asked.

"Don't be stupid," I snorted.

"I'm glad to say it's not," Auntie Joan said. "Now this is the last room. What do you think of this one, Jess?"

I stepped in. It was a bit smaller than my room in Gillingham, but had loads more character. There was an open fireplace on one side which was painted sky blue, the same as the wardrobe. The wallpaper had an ancient flowery pattern, but actually there was something about it that I liked. It belonged. And strangely, I was beginning to feel that I belonged there, too. The window opposite looked out on to the back garden – it was the most amazing view I had ever seen. Nothing but flowers and trees and grass and fields and sky, going on for ever.

Most of the room was taken up by a single iron bedstead, painted white with brass knobs. The only other furniture was a wooden bedside cabinet, and a white wicker chair under the window. I can't explain it, but I fell in love with it right away. I could picture Rodney sitting on the chair. He would love it here, and would be able to look through the window at the garden and fields beyond when I was at school. Right now, back in Gillingham, he only had the backs of the opposite terrace and the row of garages to look at.

"This was my old room when mother and father were alive," said Auntie Joan with a soft smile. "It was always a happy room."

"What do you think of it, Jess?" Mum asked, squeezing into the room. She sounded a bit anxious, and I knew why.

I didn't answer for a minute, but my heart was beating fast. I couldn't lie. I liked the room, but it was more than that. It sounds stupid, but it was like it was all meant to be. "I like it," I said. "There's just about enough room for someone to sleep on the floor. Isobel and me could take turns at who has the bed."

"You can have this one then," said Brendan, "when we move."

Mum smiled. "Well, we'll need to discuss it first."

"There's nothing to discuss, Mum," I said. "Brendan wants to move, so do you, I know you do. And now I've seen this room, I do, too."

"Well that's good then," said Brendan. "Can we see the garden now? I'm going to bring my football goal, so I need to know where to put it."

Mum ignored him; she was still looking at me, amazed. "Are you sure? I thought you said you needed more time to think about it."

"I'm sure," I said, and gave her a hug. "This will be a new start for all of us."

"You're right," Mum said, "but I didn't want to force anything on either of you. I'm ready for something different, though. I'd like to come and take up Auntie Joan's offer. At least try it out, see if she can put up with us. You're obviously happy with the idea, Brendan?"

"Yes, I can't wait to see the garden. Can we move next week?"

"I think that might be a bit too soon," said Auntie Joan, but she was smiling as if she was really pleased. "Your mother will have a lot of sorting and packing to do," she continued. "I think we should all go down and have lunch, and discuss the details."

"You've got your holiday with Dexter coming up, anyway," Mum reminded him.

"Oh yeah. What's for lunch?" asked Brendan, thinking of his stomach as usual.

Auntie Joan smiled. "If I'm not badly mistaken, all young people like pizza. Is that right?"

"Right, Auntie Joan," I said, and before I knew what I was doing, I'd put my arm round her shoulder. *This old lady's going to be OK to live with*, I thought.

At the foot of the stairs leading down from my room was a large dining room, with a piano at one end, and a massive, old-fashioned table and chairs at the other. As we entered it, Auntie Joan said, "I've ordered two deep-pan pizzas from Sittingbourne, and hopefully that's the delivery man I can hear coming down the lane on his motorcycle."

"It is!" shouted Brendan, running to open the front door and it wasn't long before we were all seated round the dining table with the pizzas on big white plates in the middle.

"I always like to begin a meal by giving thanks to God," said Auntie Joan, as Brendan was about to grab a slice. "Will you join me?"

I looked at Mum, who signalled with a look that we should respect Auntie Joan's wish, and bowed her head slightly. The two of us followed suit but made faces at each other while Auntie Joan had her eyes closed. I hoped my decision was the right one, and we hadn't enrolled in a convent.

After a few minutes of silent eating, Mum spoke up. "So, what exactly will you want me to do, Auntie Joan?" she asked.

"Nothing too demanding, I hope. I shall need you to look after the housework, and I don't think I shall be up to cooking for a family. But to be frank, Tracy, I would like you to come here as much to be company for me, as to do the work. I don't know what it is because I've been on my own for years, but suddenly I feel like this cottage is too quiet."

"Obviously we don't know each other well yet," Mum said, "but from what I've heard and seen this morning, I don't think we'll have too much trouble getting on."

Auntie Joan smiled and looked round at us all. "That's exactly my feeling," she agreed, which was a relief. After all, she might have been having second thoughts about having us to live with her, now she'd met us!

"Jess and Brendan make quite a bit of noise," Mum warned, and we grinned at each other.

"As I said, this house has been too quiet for too many years. A bit of noise will do these walls some good. I shall want to pay you of course, Tracy."

"You said that in your letter. Thank you very much. This is all beginning to seem like a fairytale. I hope it's all for real."

"Tracy, I assure you this is all for real. What about you, Jess and Brendan, what do you think?"

"I think coming here's a brilliant idea," Brendan said, helping himself to another slice of pizza. "I can't wait. Living in the country will be fun! Mum, can we have chickens? And you'll have enough money to buy me some new football boots."

"I've already said what I think," I said. I could have added that I was apprehensive about losing my friends, especially Isobel, and moving schools, but saying goodbye to Alice and her bullying buddies would be a huge relief. I left all that out though.

"When would you like us to move in, Auntie Joan?" Mum asked. "I'll need to contact the landlord."

"What about the end of August? You'll need to sort out schools, as well as all the packing. Do you think that's too soon?"

"That sounds perfect. Jess and Brendan, you're going to have to help me with sorting out the house though," she warned.

"I will," Brendan said.

"You can count on me," I said. Now that I – we – had made up our minds to move, I couldn't do it soon enough.

"I don't think you'll regret the decision," Auntie Joan said, "but at the same time, there are a few weeks before you come. If you do change your minds, I shall be disappointed, but I shan't hold it against you. I want what's best for all of you, as well as what's right for me."

"May I have another slice of pizza, please, Auntie Joan?" Brendan asked.

"Ah, yes, back to the important things, Brendan!" she replied with a smile. "Then after lunch we're expecting a visitor. Actually," she added, looking at her watch, "he'll be here any minute!"

"Who?" Brendan shouted.

eleven

The Visitor

Before Auntie Joan had time to reply, the doorbell rang. "Shall I answer it, Auntie Joan?" I said, jumping up.

"Please do, I'd completely lost track of the time. It will be Aidan."

"Who's Aidan?" Brendan asked, but I missed Auntie Joan's reply because I was on my way to the front door. I opened the door to find a boy of about my own age standing there. He was taller than me, with curly ginger hair and freckles. He was clearly surprised that it was me who answered the door.

"Hi, I'm Aidan," he said. "You must be Jess?"

"Do come in, Aidan," Auntie Joan said from behind me. "I'm afraid I hadn't got around to warning my guests you were coming."

We all crowded into the dining room. "I'm Tracy, Joan's niece," Mum said.

"And I'm Brendan."

"Sit yourself down a minute, Aidan, please," Auntie Joan said. "We're just finishing lunch. Brendan is that the last slice? I thought you might like someone to show you young people a little bit of the village, so I invited Aidan to come round."

I cringed inside and felt sorry for him as well as us – how embarrassing to be asked to look after us. Still, he looked normal enough.

"There's not a lot to show you," Aidan admitted.

"You're not trying to put them off coming here, are you, Aidan?" Mum said with a smile.

He grinned back. "No, I like it here! What time do you need us to be back?"

"Oh, I think four o'clock would be good," said Auntie Joan. "There's no rush."

"OK, we'll have a quick look round the village, and then we can chill out at my place."

Auntie Joan nodded. "That's lovely, dear. It will give Tracy and I a chance to chat about some of the more boring practicalities of the move."

"Are you definitely going to move here, then?" Aidan asked, as we walked back down the hall, after we'd said goodbye.

"Yes," Brendan said, "We were just waiting for Jess to make up her mind."

"That's not fair!" I said.

"It's true," Brendan said, and I didn't reply, because he was right, really.

Brendan and I followed Aidan out of the front door, and started down the short lane towards the main road, then we crossed over to enter the churchyard through a small gate. We walked up the path between gravestones. It was warm and sunny, and birds were singing. It was like being on holiday.

"Auntie Joan's sister is buried here somewhere near a big beech tree. Do you think we could find her gravestone?" I asked. "She would have been our other great-aunt."

"Sure," said Aidan, pointing out the tree. "By the way, there are owls living in the churchyard, so you might hear them at night."

"Cool," said Brendan. "I hope I get to see them as well as hear them."

"Does anyone actually go to this church, Aidan?" I asked, looking up at the massive structure.

"Loads of people. So do I, with my mum and dad, every week," he said.

"Every week?" Brendan repeated in amazement. "Why?"

"Isn't it boring?" I asked. "All those old hymns and stuff?"

"We sing a lot of modern songs as well," Aidan said, "but church is not so much about going to a building, as the people in it. Some of my friends go, too."

Mm, I thought. *Was there a God conspiracy going on?* I didn't say anything, because at that point we found Sybil's gravestone. It said:

Sacred to the memory of Sybil Doreen Armstrong
Departed this life 7th October 1962

There were six red roses in a little pot on the grave. "Auntie Joan must have put those flowers there," I said. "It's very sad."

Aidan nodded. "It is, if death is all there is."

"I don't believe there's life after death," I said.

He just smiled, and I tried not to curl my lip. Still, he was welcome to waste his Sunday mornings going to church if he wanted.

We turned back towards the village, and left the churchyard again through a small wooden gate. "Like I said, there's not a lot to show you," Aidan said. "That pub there is *The Dog and Hen*. My grandfather used to keep that; Mum grew up there. Grandad lives in Sittingbourne now. Let's go down The Street."

"Which street?" I asked.

"It's just called The Street," Aidan said with a grin. "It's the main road, but there are only two shops. There used to be a Post Office, but it closed."

"Is there a park?" Brendan asked hopefully.

"Right after these cottages," Aidan said. A small green metal gate led up a short path between shrubs to a play area with a set of swings and a roundabout.

"Is that all?" asked Brendan, looking a bit disappointed.

"Sorry," Aidan said, "I guess it's a bit of a let-down after Gillingham, but there are some bigger play areas in Sittingbourne."

It certainly was quiet – we'd hardly seen anyone. We walked to the end of The Street, passing a butcher's and a convenience store, then the road took a bend to the left through woodland to become the road leading down to Sittingbourne.

"That's about all there is," Aidan said.

There was a clear look of disappointment on Brendan's face, and I thought it was probably because he'd been so adamant that he wanted to move that he didn't say anything.

"We'll go back a bit, and my house is in The Close on the right," Aidan said.

He led the way. The Close consisted of about ten houses that were a lot more modern than Auntie Joan's. "Do you want a game of pool?" Aidan said, as we walked up the path to his front door. "We've got a pool table in our garage."

"I've never played it," I admitted.

"It's pretty simple," Aidan said. "You'll pick up the rules quickly."

"Can I play as well?" Brendan said.

"We'll take turns," Aidan replied. "I'll just tell Mum we're back." But he didn't need to, because she came to the door as we got there. She was rather short with a round face and flushed cheeks, and red curly hair, like Aidan.

"You must be Jess and Brendan," she said. "Welcome! Joan said you were stopping for the weekend."

"We've decided to stop a lot longer than that," I said. "We're all going to move here in a few weeks."

"That's great news!" she said. "It'll do Joan good to have company, and I think you'll find she's easy to get on with. I'm Jennifer, by the way."

"Mum, we're going to have a game of pool," Aidan said, as we all trooped through the house to the kitchen at the back. A fabulous smell of baking greeted us.

"OK," Jennifer said. "I made some blueberry muffins while you were out, so help yourselves."

"Yum!" said Brendan, his mood noticeably brightening, and we all grabbed a muffin as we went through the back door and into the garage. There was a small green car on one side, and the pool table on the other.

"Dad parks his work van on the drive so we can have the pool table in here," Aidan said, getting a box of balls off the shelf and picking up two cues from a rack.

"Your mum and dad must be very rich for you to afford a car and a van," Brendan said. "We don't even have one car."

"I guess we are pretty well off," Aidan said, "I don't think we're super-rich though. Dad's a builder; Mum does all the accounts and stuff."

"My dad was a bricklayer before, but..." then I stopped. I wondered how much Auntie Joan had told Aidan about our family, and what he would think if he knew about Dad.

"How do we play pool?" asked Brendan, grabbing one of the cues from Aidan. "Do we shoot with these sticks?"

"The sticks are called cues," Aidan said with a grin, "and, yes, you shoot the balls with the cues."

"All the balls are different colours," Brendan said. "Which one do you hit first?"

"The balls that have stripes are called *stripes*, and the other balls are *solids*," Aidan explained, gathering all the balls together. "First we get all the balls inside this triangle. The white ball is the cue ball. The first player to shoot makes what's called the break. If he or she hits, say, a stripe into a pocket, he's on stripes and the other player has to go for the solids. Each player then tries to pocket all their balls."

"Can I go first?" asked Brendan.

"OK, you can play against me first, then you and Jess can play each other."

Brendan's first attempt at hitting the cue ball sent it flying all of three inches. On his second go, it bounced right over the edge of the table.

"That's what we call a *scratch*," Aidan told us with a grin. Brendan soon managed to pocket a solid, and after a bit of tuition, we were both soon getting the feel of how to hold the cue and send the cue ball in the direction we wanted. It was actually quite a laugh, and we had four or five games, taking turns.

"You'll need to check out the schools in Sittingbourne, Jess," Aidan said while we played. "What year will you be in, in September?"

"Year Nine."

"Same as me. It would be great if you were able to get into my school! You can check out the others though."

"I know. I already started to, but I wasn't doing it very seriously, because I didn't really want to live here."

"Mum and me wanted to though," Brendan interrupted.

"What changed your mind?" Aidan asked me.

I paused for a minute. "OK, this is going to sound weird. I really liked the bedroom Auntie Joan offered me, and I like Auntie Joan, too, but it's more than that. It's like it was meant to be."

As soon as I said that I bit my tongue in case Aidan came out with something religious again, but he only grinned and said, "Everyone likes Joan."

"Talking of Auntie Joan, what time is it?" I asked. "It must be nearly time to be getting back."

"It's quarter to four," Aidan said, checking his phone, "so we ought to be packing up. What about you, Brendan, how old are you?"

"Nine and a half," he said.

"You'll probably go to the primary school in the village, then. It's only small, but I think you'll like it. I did. The teachers are really nice."

"Good," said Brendan.

"You can join the village youth club, Jess," Aidan said. "It's every Friday in the church hall, and we play pool there, and table tennis and other games."

"Auntie Joan already suggested that," I said. "Where is the church hall?"

"Sorry, I should have shown you that. It's just the other side of the church."

"I'll think about it," I said. I wanted to meet the other young people in the village, but I was a bit nervous in case they were posh, boring, or religious, or were snobby to us cos of our dad.

twelve

Brendan Has a Fright

"I do hope you'll all be warm enough tonight," Auntie Joan said after we'd finished our hot chocolate that evening.

"Don't worry, Auntie Joan," I said. "If anything, we'll be too warm, with these summer nights." And then I surprised myself when I gave her a hug as Brendan and me got up to go to our rooms.

Auntie Joan smiled. "Sleep well! I'll be going to the early service at church in the morning, but you know where the kitchen is now, so just help yourselves to cereal and toast if I'm not here when you get up."

"Goodnight, Jess. Goodnight, Brendan," Mum said, and we both gave her a hug, too. I can't explain it, but it was like the stress of the last few weeks was beginning to melt away. I could see it in Mum's face as I felt it in my own.

Brendan and I both went up the flight of stairs that led from the front door. Brendan carried on up to his room, and I went along the landing to mine. "Don't wake me up too early, Jess," said Brendan, with a big yawn.

"No way will I be up early; it's Sunday tomorrow. Hope the owls don't scare you in the night."

"It would take more than an owl to frighten me," he said. "Night, Jess."

"Night Brendan."

An evening breeze had got up and the window in my room rattled a bit. I wondered how cold the room would get in the winter. After changing into my pjs, I turned off the light and got in under the blanket and quilt. They felt heavy, so I tossed the quilt onto the floor.

There was a half-moon and a beam of light shone between the curtains. Then I heard a scratching noise. I listened; it seemed to be coming from the door. I got out of bed, tripping over my bag, and opened the door a fraction. "Brendan?" I whispered, but a wet nose and whiskers pushed through the gap. It was Bernard! I was surprised he wasn't keeping clear of strangers; instead he was clearly intent on getting to know his new guest. I opened the door fully so he could get in, and he immediately jumped up on my bed and began to purr.

I got under the blanket again. After a bit of a cuddle, Bernard settled down at the bottom of my bed, and I moved him over to one side with my feet. As I lay there in the quiet, I reflected on the day – one that was about to change the whole course of my life. I was about to exchange the town for the country, and leave everything I had ever known behind me, yet I had a strong feeling that this was where I now belonged. I fell asleep to the sound of the wind outside, and Bernard purring.

I didn't often dream, but that night I did. Brendan was climbing up a church tower, and he was in danger. I was frantically following him. It was a spiral staircase, and no matter how far I climbed he was always somewhere ahead, out of sight. Then suddenly there was a loud crash, and the sound of Brendan hurtling down the stairs. "Jess!" he called, "Jess! Help me, I'm scared. Jess!"

Something struck my face. "Get off me!" I screamed.

"Jess! Wake up! It's me, Brendan!"

I woke to realise Brendan was tapping my cheek. "Brendan, what are you doing?" I asked, as my brain started to come to. "Where am I?" and then remembered I was in my new room at Auntie Joan's. "Brendan, what are you doing here? Why aren't you in your bed?"

74

Mum came to the door. "Jess, Brendan, what on earth's going on? I heard a crash, and Brendan running downstairs. Then it must have been the cat running along the landing into Auntie Joan's room, and next there was all this shouting."

"My bed collapsed," Brendan said.

"You must have weakened it yesterday when you jumped on it," Mum said.

"The bed collapsed, and it woke me up," he said. "Then I heard a weird squawking noise. I stood up and looked out of the window, and I could see lights moving. I think the noise was coming from the same place as the lights."

"Don't be daft, Brendan," I said, finally coming round. "It's your imagination."

"It's not. I tell you I saw all these lights moving about."

"You probably heard the church owl," I said.

"Owls hoot, they don't squawk," Mum said. "But whatever you heard or saw, it's time you got back to sleep. You can use the other bed. You've probably woken Auntie Joan up; she'll be coming to see what's going on."

"I'm not sleeping in that room. I'm scared," Brendan said.

Mum sighed. "You'd better bring your blankets down, then, and sleep on the floor."

"You can sleep on the rug next to my bed," I said, just wanting to get back to sleep.

"All right then, I will," said Brendan, "but I did see lights."

"Just do it quietly," Mum whispered, going back to her bedroom.

Brendan went up to his room and gathered his bedding, and was soon settled on the floor beside me. "I did see lights, Jess," he said in a half whisper.

"OK, Brendan, we get the message," I said. "Now just go to sleep, please." In a few minutes Brendan was breathing regularly and I must have dropped off eventually, because when I next opened my eyes, the sun was shining brightly through the curtains, and Brendan had already got up and left the room.

thirteen

Tyre Tracks

"Jennifer asked after you both," Auntie Joan said at the lunch table later that day, after saying her prayer as usual. "She said I was blessed to have two such polite children coming to live with me. And Aidan told me you were both welcome to go round to play pool any time. He hasn't got any brothers or sisters, so he'd probably appreciate the company."

"OK, thanks," I said.

"It's such a pleasure to have a meal all cooked for me, and family to eat with," added Auntie Joan, looking round at us, and at the plates of roast beef and vegetables. "A lovely treat indeed."

You'd think we'd done her a massive favour, but she'd paid for it all! Mum had cooked roast beef whilst Auntie Joan was out at the church, and I'd helped with the veg. The smell of everything cooking had been making me feel hungry for hours.

"It's a nice change for us to have roast beef," Mum said. "My budget doesn't run to beef. It's usually chicken or sausages."

"Beef's my favourite," said Brendan, cramming a massive piece in his mouth.

"Well, Brendan, you enjoy your roast beef," said Auntie Joan with a smile.

"You wait till you try Mum's cakes," said Brendan. "They're the best ever. By the way, did you hear my bed crash, in the night Auntie Joan? I'm sorry about that."

"Yes, it did wake me up. I'd have tried to help, but I could hear your mother was already sorting it out."

"It wasn't really my fault."

"It was! You must have cracked the bed, yesterday," I said.

"It was an old bed, in any case," Auntie Joan said. "Let's not fret about it. We'll see about getting a new one as soon as you move in. You can choose the one you like, Brendan. By the way, did any of you hear vehicles soon after the crash?"

"No, I didn't," I said. "We were too busy listening to Brendan."

"There were several that went through the village, which is very strange at that time of night."

"There's nothing very odd about that, is there?" I said. "It's normal for our part of Gillingham."

"But not for Millhurst," Auntie Joan said. "Once *The Dog and Hen* has closed, there are not usually many cars on the move. And definitely not several all together."

"A mystery!" I said. "So living in a village isn't dull then? As it's sunny outside," I added, looking out the window, "can we go out after lunch? Do some exploring?"

"After you and Brendan have done the dishes," Mum said.

"Do we have to, Mum?" Brendan said. "What's for afters?"

"Auntie Joan had bought some cooking apples," Mum said. "So I've baked an apple tart."

"With cream?" I asked.

"Yes, with cream."

"Great! Double great!" Brendan said.

"I can see the man who comes round with the grocery van is going to be delighted at the up-turn in trade," said Aunt Joan with a smile. "As for Jess's idea, I think we should explore the fields behind the cottage once we've cleared everything away."

So, an hour or so later all four of us walked through the back garden and out of an old wooden gate, which joined a path leading into a series of large fields. Some of the fields were just grass, others were sown with crops. In the distance we could see a few houses, but apart from that, all you could see was the countryside.

We hadn't gone far, though, when Auntie Joan stopped and looked at some muddy tyre tracks in the field. "I'm trying to work out what all these are," she said.

"Maybe the farmer's been driving round the field?" suggested Brendan.

"These are car tyres," Auntie Joan said. "The farmer would have come in his tractor."

"There are several different patterns," I said, examining the markings. Some tracks were a series of little Vs, others were lines of various widths.

"There must have been several vehicles here!" said Auntie Joan. "Whatever were they doing?"

"And there's lots of white feathers on the ground," I said, noticing a pile of them a few paces further on.

"So there are," she said. "Well I never. And there are more next to the hedge, look!" We all followed Auntie Joan, who was already striding off to investigate.

"Do you know what kind of feathers these are, Auntie Joan?" I asked.

"They're chicken feathers," she said.

"What are they doing here, then?" I said. "We haven't passed a farm, or anywhere with chickens."

"I'm asking myself the same question. I haven't seen anything like this for years, but there were clearly lots of vehicles here, and as well as the feathers, there are streaks of blood on the ground."

Mum came up to us. "Are you thinking what I think you are, Auntie Joan?" she asked.

"What do you mean, Mum?" asked Brendan. "Is it a mystery?"

"This could be the scene of cockfighting," Mum said.

"What's cockfighting?" we both asked at the same time.

"It's a very cruel business, that some people call sport," Mum said. "It's when they put two cockerels together so that they fight one another, and they usually tie something sharp like a razor blade to the cockerels' feet so that they injure one another. They let them fight until one of them is killed."

Brendan's mouth dropped open and I screwed up my face. "That's disgusting!" I said, then I had a sudden thought. "I wonder if there's any connection between the lights that Brendan claims to have seen, the vehicles that Auntie Joan heard, and all these tyre tracks?"

"I *did* see lights!" Brendan insisted. "And I heard squawking. I told you but you didn't believe me."

81

"The lights you saw might have been from the cars that were here," reflected Auntie Joan. "The window in your bedroom does face this way. It looks like there might have been a cockfight taking place right here!"

"And the noises you heard, Brendan, could have been the cockerels," Mum said.

"Wow, that's scary," he said, making a face.

Auntie Joan pursed her lips. "And it's against the law," she said. "We'll need to report all this to the police when we get back."

We returned to the footpath and carried on walking. As we walked, Auntie Joan pointed out wild flowers and different birds we saw on the way. She knew her stuff when it came to nature, but all the while I kept thinking about the cockfighting and how the poor birds must have suffered. The walk wasn't fun any more, despite Auntie Joan's nature commentary, and we all kept coming back to the same subject.

"How could people be so cruel?" I asked.

Auntie Joan shook her head. "I don't know. It's beyond me how anyone could find enjoyment in seeing a bird or an animal in pain."

We were all feeling upset about the cockerels, and eventually Mum said, "I think we ought to turn round now. We'll need to get our things together ready for going home, and we should let Auntie Joan phone the police and tell them what we've seen."

"I quite agree, Tracy," Auntie Joan said. You've time for a cup of tea and some cake before you go, though?"

"I don't want to go back to Gillingham," Brendan said with a pout. "This feels like home already. And I want to get the people who did the cockfighting and make them pay for their crime."

I rolled my eyes at the last bit, but I knew what he meant, both about the cockerels, and about feeling at home. It was strange. It seemed as if Millhurst and Auntie Joan's cottage were already becoming home.

As we packed up our stuff ready for the taxi, I wondered whatever would happen next. I was starting to feel a freedom that I can't explain. It was as though, somehow, living in Gillingham had confined and restricted me, but now I was being set free. And it didn't seem like living in a village was going to be boring, either!

fourteen

Moving Out

"Where do you want me to put your trainers?" asked Isobel.

"In the brown bag," I said.

"And what about your dirty socks?"

"Just stuff them in as well. I'll put them in the washing machine at the new house." My room was looking a complete tip. The wardrobe doors hung open; there were just a couple of school shirts and a canary-yellow fleece on hangers, and my winter boots were at the bottom. Mum had given me some boxes, a big brown bag with a broken zip, and a rather battered suitcase that had last been used a few years ago when we had money and had holidays. The bedroom floor was littered with magazines, shoes, books, and three bulging black bin bags.

"The brown bag's full already," Isobel said, as she

tried to squeeze the trainers and socks in one end, whilst a blue sweat-shirt started spewing out at the other end.

"The suitcase is full, too," I sighed. "I tell you what, I'll pull the zip closed, while you sit on it. That's how they do it in films."

We did just that; only the seam burst apart on one corner. We both burst out, too – into laughter! "Oh no!" I said. "That would happen. I've got so much stuff! Never mind. It'll have to do like that."

"Jess, there's nowhere for Rodney," Isobel said.

"He can come in the taxi with me."

"Have you got room for all of this stuff in your new place?"

"Not really. Mine's the smallest room, with just one wardrobe."

"Perhaps you need to downsize," Isobel said. That's what my gran did when she moved into her apartment."

"Yeah, Mum keeps telling me to get rid of stuff I don't use any more. I suppose I am a bit of a hoarder."

"Jess, you know I'm going to miss you so much." Isobel said, her eyes beginning to fill up. "Do you have to go?"

"You know I do," I said. "I shall miss you, too, and I shall miss everyone at school. To be honest, I'm trying not to think about that side of it. When Mum first got Auntie Joan's letter, I felt like everything was slipping away from me. Dad had gone, and it looked as if I was about to lose my home and everything else as well."

"And now?"

I stopped to think. "It's like we have this opportunity we've got to grab now or we'll lose it forever."

"Does your mum really want to be a cleaner? It doesn't sound much of an opportunity to me."

"Well, Auntie Joan said Mum would be more of a companion than a cleaner. Even though Aunt Joan's ancient, she's fun. You'll have to come and meet her, as soon as you can, yeah?"

"Living in a big rambling house sounds fun," Isobel said. "And I love the countryside."

"Yeah, I'm getting excited about moving. I've been thinking about that cockfighting thing, too. I'm thinking I might start some sort of campaign."

"If the people who are doing it know that it's wrong, they're not going to take much notice of you standing there with a poster saying Care for our Cockerels."

"Well, yes," I said, "but there must be something I can do."

"You'll have to catch the people red-handed," Isobel said, "but that would be dangerous. Jess you won't do anything risky, will you?"

I laughed. "No, of course not!"

"It's bad enough that you're moving away; I don't want anything to happen to you."

"Stop worrying, I'll be OK," I said, "and as for moving away, Sittingbourne's not that far. You can get the bus there."

"Soon, I hope."

"Soon as we can fix it up. Remember, Auntie Joan said you can come and stay any time."

"In the middle of all these bags?" Isobel said with a grin.

"There will always be space for you! What's the time? Mum's taking us out to McDonald's with the money she got from selling our kitchen stuff."

"It's half twelve!"

"OK, let's go!"

fifteen

Moving In

"Mind my hand!" I snapped. "You're squashing it between the box and the wall."

"You should watch where you're going," Brendan retorted. "I'm having to walk up the stairs backwards. I can't take care of you as well."

I was exhausted with moving my boxes and bags from our new living room where the removals man had dumped them. "I'm tired," I said.

"Me, too." Brendan replied. "This is the fifth time we've come upstairs with your stuff. I only had two bags."

"That's because you're always chucking things away," I said, wiping the sweat off my forehead with the back of my bruised hand.

"And you wouldn't have so much stuff if you didn't hold on to everything." Just as we reached my bedroom door one of the boxes split, and my leather boots, jeans and DVDs spilled out on to the floor. Bernard had been hiding under the bed. He shot out and ran down the stairs – well, more of a fast waddle.

"Brendan, that's your fault," I said, annoyed.

"I couldn't help it. This doorway's so narrow." He picked up the jeans, and threw them on the wicker chair.

"Not on top of Rodney!" I said, lifting the jeans off Rodney's head, and sitting him straight again.

"Anyway," Brendan said. "Auntie Joan said we're leaving for Sittingbourne at three o'clock to buy me a new bed. That's in five minutes, if you want to come. We're going in her Beetle."

"Her what?" I asked.

"Beetle. Volkswagen Beetle, it's a type of old car."

"That's a silly name for a car."

"It's ancient. I'm glad Dexter's not here to see me going in it."

The car did look a bit like a bug, and it was orange. But it was better than getting the bus, even if Auntie Joan didn't drive faster than twenty-five miles an hour all the way. With her wearing thick glasses, I hoped she could see all right.

We parked in the centre of town, near the high street, which was made up of all kinds of small shops and offices – it would be fun to explore them with Isobel one day, I decided.

A salesman in a suit and tie came up to us in the furniture shop. "May I help you?" he asked Auntie Joan, politely.

"We're looking for a single divan bed, please," she said.

The man led us to a row of beds.

"Which one do you fancy, Brendan?" Auntie Joan asked.

"I thought we'd have to buy the cheapest one," he said, looking surprised.

"No dear, you can choose," said Auntie Joan.

Brendan looked up and down the row of beds, "I like this one with the red mattress," he said.

"You don't see the mattress once the bedding's on it," I scoffed.

"Would you like to lie on it?" the salesman asked him.

"Lie on it?" Brendan repeated, once more looking surprised.

"Perhaps you should take your shoes off, Brendan," Auntie Joan suggested with a smile.

Brendan didn't need to be asked twice. He lay on that bed, and tried bouncing on it a bit. "This one's amazing."

"It has a high quality memory foam mattress," the assistant said in a rather pompous tone. "It has a five year guarantee."

"Do you want to try any others, Brendan?" Auntie Joan asked, so he lay on all of them, and I tried them as well, to help him choose.

"I still like the first one," Brendan decided eventually.

So Auntie Joan sorted out payment and delivery, and as we stepped out of the shop she said, "Now then Jess and Brendan, I've got a little shopping to do before we head back home. But first, I'm ready for a cup of tea." She pointed out a café on the other side of the road. "Shall we go over there? You could both have a doughnut, if you like, and something to drink."

"Do they do milkshakes?" asked Brendan.

"I think so," Auntie Joan replied. "Shall we go and see?" On the way we passed a newsagent. Outside was a placard with a headline written in big letters with a black felt-tip pen.

POLICE HUNT FOR COCKFIGHTING GANG

I gasped and pointed it out. "Look at that, Auntie Joan! The police are still looking for the cockfighting gang!"

91

"I know," she said. "I was reading about it in the paper last week. It said the gang keeps holding the fights in different locations in Kent."

"Did the police look at the car tracks we found?" I asked.

"Yes, I believe they took lots of photographs."

"May be I can set a trap to catch the gang," suggested Brendan.

"That doesn't sound very realistic," I replied.

"It sounds, from what the police are saying, that they don't go back to the same place twice," Auntie Joan said, "but we can keep our eyes open, of course."

"I hope the police catch those criminals, before any more cockerels are killed," I said.

"Me too," agreed Brendan, with feeling. Over our doughnuts and milkshakes, Auntie Joan asked how we were feeling about the move.

"I'm a bit nervous about my new school," I said, "but Millhurst feels like home already." Brendan nodded agreement.

"I am glad," Auntie Joan said, "but I do want you to tell me if there's anything you're unhappy about."

"What about you, Auntie Joan?" I asked. "It must feel like your house has been invaded by an army, after living on your own for so many years."

"To be frank, I'm wishing I'd done this a long time ago. To really feel part of a family again makes me feel younger, somehow. It's like a new start, as if life has more purpose."

I looked across the table at her, and was glad. There was something warm and comforting about her that I couldn't remember feeling about anyone else before. My life no longer felt so overshadowed by the tension between Mum and Dad; life seemed more peaceful.

But then I remembered the cockerels again, cooped up in some cage somewhere, probably badly kept in a dirty backyard, and unaware that soon they would be pitted against other unfortunate birds and engaged in a bloody fight until one of them was dead.

It made me feel ill. They were like prisoners awaiting execution, with no one to stand up for them, no one to help them get free. Here was I, free from Alice Davies and her gang of bullies. Was there anything I could do to help set the cockerels free?

sixteen

First Day at School

The first morning of the new term, Auntie Joan dropped me off at the school gates. "Are you sure you don't want me to come in with you?" she asked.

"No, I'll be all right on my own, but thanks for offering." I smiled, as I stepped out of the car.

I'd been instructed to report to Mrs Streeter, the Head of Year, on the first floor. I'd already met her the day I came with Mum to be interviewed. I was a bit self-conscious as I made my way to her room and knocked on her door.

"Come in! Oh, hello Jess, welcome! I expect you're feeling anxious."

"Good morning, Mrs Streeter. Yes, I am a bit."

"Well, we're a friendly school. You'll soon get used to us. I've tried to make sure you've got all you need, but I'm bound to have forgotten something, so don't be afraid to come and ask me, or your form tutor, Miss Grant."

"Thank you," I said, forcing a nervous smile.

"Miss Grant is new, too, so maybe you can help each other settle in," she said. That was a comforting thought: I wasn't the only one who was new.

"Where do we go for lunch?" I asked.

"The cafeteria is on the other side of the science block; through the double blue doors."

"Oh, I saw them on my way in," I said.

"Good. I've asked Elena Craig, in your class, to show you round and keep an eye on you during the first couple of days till you're familiar with everything. You're in the same set as her for most subjects."

"Thank you," I said. It was good to know that I wasn't being left to my own devices.

"Your form room is B7. Let's go in and I'll introduce you to Miss Grant, and hopefully Elena will have arrived already."

About a dozen students were already in the tutor room, exchanging tales about the summer holidays. I stood out straight away because my dark green uniform was completely new; everyone else's had been around for a couple of years. Aidan was sitting at a desk near the window with another boy, who was showing him something on his phone. Aidan must have heard Mrs Streeter's voice; he looked up and waved.

Miss Grant was filling out some forms at her desk, but stood up to greet Mrs Streeter and me.

"I'll leave you now, Jess," Mrs Streeter said. "There's a notepad hanging on the door of my office, and if I'm out I always write where I've gone, so you can come and find me. I hope you're happy with us here, and quickly feel part of the school family." She turned and left the room.

Miss Grant was young, with short auburn hair, and was wearing a smart grey suit. "So you've just moved from Gillingham," she said. "I don't think you'll find it too different here. I shall be teaching you French. Do you like languages?"

"Yes, I do. I did French and Spanish at my old school. Some of my friends have been abroad, but apart from one day in Calais, I've never been out of England."

"Never mind, you can still learn to speak a foreign language quite well. The school has installed a new language laboratory over the summer, which I think you'll find helpful. How did you get on with science in your school in Gillingham?"

"It wasn't my best subject."

"Well if you need any help, just ask."

"OK," I said, feeling a bit worried that I might look really thick. "I realise I'm going to have to work at making friends, too."

"I quite agree, and if you are struggling, come and tell me. You may find it helpful to join one or two of the after-school clubs. They're a good way to make friends."

I was already feeling happier. It seemed like the teachers really cared, and wanted to help me settle in quickly. Elena had seen me come in to the room, and came over to Miss Grant's desk. "Elena will take good care of you," Miss Grant said. "I could have done with a buddy myself last week; I kept going up one floor too many!"

"Hi, Jess. You're going to be sitting next to me," Elena said. "We're in the same sets for everything except music and dancing. Let me show you where your locker is."

"Thank you, Elena," said Miss Grant.

"Hope you have a good first day, Jess."

"I hope you do, too, Miss."

She smiled back. "Thank you!"

"Where do you live?" Elena asked me, as we set off down the corridor.

"In Millhurst," I replied.

"Oh!" she said, surprised. "Will you be getting the bus? I catch the Millhurst bus; I live on Millhurst Lane!"

"My aunt drove me in this morning, but I'll be getting the bus back tonight."

"Great!" she said with a laugh. "We can get the bus together!" The bell rang for the first lesson and everyone moved off to their classes.

The first lesson was maths, which was far from being my strong point. I struggled to understand the geometry that the teacher, Mr Berry, was going through. I could see that a lot of the students seemed to be way ahead of me, and realised with a sinking feeling that I'd got a lot of catching up to do. History was next, and the topic was whether it was right to have dropped the atomic bomb on Hiroshima, or not. We'd covered this in my old school, so I understood the arguments for both sides, and started to feel more relaxed.

As the morning wore on, everything started to feel less strange and less intimidating. I was thankful when the bell for lunch break sounded, though. All this new stuff was exhausting.

"We're supposed to go to the first sitting for lunch," Elena said. "Afterwards I'll give you a quick tour of the buildings to give you an idea of the layout of the school."

"Thanks," I said, as we made our way to the cafeteria. "Mrs Streeter showed me round when I came to register, but I'm sure I only took in half of what she said."

"You seem to be coping with your first day," Elena said. "What do you think so far?"

"Well, I'm a bit worried whether I'll be able to manage the maths; geometry never was my strongest subject."

"You're not the only one. The names are enough to put me off. Whoever thought up parallelograms and Isosceles triangles?" Elena said.

"Isosceles was Greek, wasn't he?" I said.

"Pity he wasn't British and called Fred!"

The cafeteria was busy. Aidan was sitting at another table, but when Elena and I were nearly finished, he brought two of his mates over to say hi, which was nice.

After lunch we crossed the large recreation area in the centre of the school complex. "This tall building on the left is the new sports hall," Elena said. "You said you like athletics?"

"Yes, I love running. I've missed it over the holidays."

"Mr Spencer will be pleased. He's always looking out for new talent." She opened the door of the sports hall, and I was taken aback by its size. "The Parent Teacher Association raised a lot of the money to build it," Elena explained, seeing my mouth drop open. "They only finished it last year."

"Wow," I said, "I can't wait to get in here!"

"Well, we've got gymnastics here tomorrow morning, so you haven't got long to wait." A group of Elena's friends came up to us; she was clearly very popular.

"Hi, Elena," said a tall girl with long brown hair and a friendly face.

"Hi, Naomi, this is Jess. She's just started today. Jess, this is Naomi. You can ask her about running. She's in the athletics team."

Naomi gave me a big smile. "Oh, you're Jess, I was hoping to see you!" she said. "You moved to Millhurst during the holidays, didn't you? Aidan told me on the phone last week. Are you into athletics, then?"

"I run the 200 and 300 metres."

"Great! Mr Spencer will want to give you a trial. The under-fifteens trials are after school next Tuesday. Shall I tell Mr Spencer you're coming?"

"Thank you, that would be great!" Things were going from good to better!

After Elena and I had seen the rest of the school site it was time for afternoon lessons to begin. They seemed to go much faster than the morning ones and before I knew it, the bell sounded for the end of school.

I had told Mum and Auntie Joan that I thought I'd be OK getting the bus back, and it was great to have Elena to sit next to, even if it was only for half the way. "Thanks for taking me everywhere today," I said, as she pressed the bell for her stop.

"No problem, see you tomorrow! You've got three more stops, OK? Ring the bell when you see the church tower."

I decided I'd better concentrate for the rest of the journey, or I would miss my stop, but I couldn't help my mind wandering to the athletics trials. I really hoped I'd be picked, but what if there were loads of people who were better than me?

Sittingbourne was separated from Millhurst village by a short stretch of woodland. Although it was only the beginning of September, the leaves on some of the trees were beginning to change into their autumn colours. How different this all was from my old estate! There were so many new things to get used to. But so far, they all seemed good.

seventeen

Evening at Home

I wanted to tell everyone what my first day had been like, but Brendan appeared at the front door before I'd got half way down the garden path, and came running to meet me.

"Jess, you'll never guess what happened today!" he said, jumping up and down in excitement.

"Don't tell me. Your new school caught fire?" I mocked.

"No, but a policeman and a policewoman came to our class, and told us all about cockfighting and the gang they're looking for. They asked if anyone had seen anything suspicious. I told them about the tyre tracks we'd found, but, of course, they already knew. They said we were to report anything else we saw to them or to our parents."

"I expect the gang will lie low for a little while,"

I said, "now that everyone knows the police are searching for them. Still we'll keep a look out, yeah?"

We went inside, and I dropped my bag by the front door. "Well, I'm ready to just sink into a chair," I said, doing just that, and flopping down into the armchair opposite Auntie Joan.

She smiled at me. "Tiring day, Jess?"

"Very. Everyone was really friendly, but a lot of the stuff they did last year was different from what we did at my old school, so I've got a lot of catching up to do."

"I'm sure you'll get there if you just work at it steadily."

"You're probably right," I said. "At least I knew where I was with the French and geography, and I'd done the history before."

"History was one of my best subjects at school. I'm sure I could have done it at university, but people didn't have the money in those days."

"You sound like Mum talking," I said.

"Your mother is right. I think she's an intelligent woman. Too intelligent to be a cleaner for an old lady!"

"I heard that," Mum said, coming into the room. "I'm thinking I might do some online courses in English and maths in my spare time, and maybe work towards business studies."

"Wow, way to go Mum," I said, and we high-fived. She was looking relaxed, which was good to see. "What time's dinner?"

"Six o'clock, if that suits Auntie Joan?"

"That's fine for me, Tracy," Auntie Joan agreed.

"And me," I said. "Gives me time to try to figure out my geometry homework."

"Jennifer called this morning, by the way," Mum said. "She said Aidan had invited you to the youth club at the church."

"I'll think about it," I said.

"It would be good for you to make some friends in the village. She said they're all going away for a weekend in a few weeks' time."

"OK, like I said, I'll think about it." I went up to my room. It felt like people were pushing this church thing on me. I liked Aidan, but I didn't want to be brainwashed into believing something that wasn't true.

Auntie Joan had managed to find me a little table for homework, so I propped Rodney up against my pillow while I sat on his chair. I spread my maths books out on the table and tried to work out why triangle ABC was equivalent to triangle JKL, not that I could see the point of it all.

Just as I was starting, Brendan interrupted. "Jess," he yelled out from downstairs. "Do you want to come and play football with me?"

"No," I called back. Brendan was lucky to have no homework, and have all evening to play, but I was pleased and relieved that my first day had gone well. I felt excited about the idea of the athletics trials. Would Mr Spencer pick me, or would it be like the maths where the others were better than me?

My phone rang. It was Isobel, so that was the end of the homework. It was great to hear her voice and tell her everything, but talking to her again made me feel a bit home-sick for Gillingham. Even so, I knew I wouldn't want to go back to how things had been.

eighteen

Bullying

So I got through the first few days of school, and had a quiet weekend. I avoided the youth club, and Isobel couldn't make it over, but I spent the time sorting out all my stuff in my new room. Bernard helped! He liked sleeping on my bed, so he kept me company.

The next Monday I was looking forward to getting back to school, incredible though that may sound. I was used to the bus by then, and had pretty much sussed out where everything was and how it all worked. I was even pleased with my geometry homework!

Elena dashed through the school gates as soon as she got off the bus, that Monday morning. She wanted to catch the geography teacher before school started, to book herself on a field trip before all the places were taken.

I looked about for Naomi but couldn't see her

anywhere. As I was early I decided to go to the library to look for a book my English teacher had recommended the week before. I turned a corner in the corridor just before the library. A tall blonde girl was coming the other way with a group of friends – I recognised the girl as being in another form in Year Nine. As she got close, she suddenly moved to my left and then deliberately barged into my side. I nearly lost my balance, and my bag swung down sharply on my right arm. There was a jolt of pain in my shoulder.

"Watch where you're going!" said the girl. "Oh, sorry! You've hurt yourself." Her friends all laughed, and they carried on.

I couldn't believe it. I'd just escaped from one lot of bullies. Surely this couldn't be happening again?

I opened the library door, went in and sat at the first table I came to. I got a book out of my bag and pretended to look at it. It took me a few minutes to get over the shock of being assaulted. My shoulder hurt, but the hurt was more than the pain in my shoulder. The door opened again; I looked up. It was Miss Grant.

"Good morning, Jess," she said. "Have you had a good weekend?"

"Yes, Miss Grant, thank you."

"You don't look very happy this morning," she said, stopping by my table.

"No, I just stumbled a bit in the corridor."

Miss Grant looked at me. "How did you manage that, Jess?"

"Oh, another student accidentally walked into me," I said. Miss Grant stared at me for a moment. I could tell she suspected I wasn't telling the truth, but she obviously decided not to pursue it. "How was your first week, Miss?" I asked, wanting to change the subject.

"No major slip-ups, yet, Jess, I'm glad to say. Everyone went out of their way to help me find my feet. I hope you fared as well as me?"

"Yes," I said, trying to put this morning's bad episode out of my mind. "Having Elena as a buddy was a great help."

"Good. How are the science subjects going?"

"OK, I think. Mrs Wilkinson says I just need to get over my fear – she says that I think I'm not going to grasp something, so I don't."

"I know exactly what you mean," Miss Grant said. "I used to have the same problem with chemistry, myself. From what I've seen of you so far, I think you're a very capable student, Jess. I hear you're quite an athlete, as well."

"I wouldn't say that, Miss, but I love running. Mr. Spencer will be selecting the junior athletics team this week, so I'm hoping to get in."

"I hope so, too. Now, I came here to look for a French novel, so I'd better do that. The bell will be ringing soon." I watched her for a few seconds, and thought Miss Grant was the sort of person I'd like to be. She was friendly and natural with everyone – unassuming, yet quietly confident. Maybe I should train as a teacher – a sports teacher perhaps?

The rest of the day went well; I understood more of the geometry lesson than last time, but after that grim start, I didn't feel as relaxed. At lunchtime I sat with Elena and Naomi.

"Naomi, you see those girls sitting under the clock?" I asked. "Do you know the name of the blonde one?"

Naomi turned her head in the direction I'd indicated. "That's Harriet Coutts; she's in Form 9A. Why are you asking?"

"She banged in to me on purpose this morning, and tried to knock me down. My shoulder's still hurting."

"Just ignore her," Elena said. "She's trying to wind you up. Make her think you don't care."

"But I do care, and I'm planning on finding a way to get my own back."

"She'll only make trouble for you, Jess," Naomi warned. "Just leave it."

"I was bullied at my last school; I'm not having it start all over again."

Naomi pursed her lips. "You could speak to Miss Grant, or Mrs Streeter?"

"No, I'll handle it myself. I'll find a way of teaching her a lesson."

"You'd better be careful," she said, "or you'll be the one getting into trouble."

Elena nodded agreement. "I think Naomi's right," she said. "If you ignore her she'll go away."

"I did that at my last school, and it didn't work," I said, and I looked at Harriet giggling amongst her friends.

I'll teach you a lesson before I've finished, I thought.

nineteen

Athletics Trials

On the day of the athletics trials the weather was miserable. The skies were leaden grey, and it drizzled all morning. It was still raining during the lunch break. I was afraid the trials would be postponed, but during the last period of the afternoon the rain stopped, and a few breaks appeared in the clouds. It was a history lesson, which is a subject I normally enjoy, although I don't often achieve high marks when it comes to tests. I struggled to concentrate on a discussion about the long-term effects of the Cold War, though, as I kept my eye on the clouds.

At last the bell rang. I quickly gathered up my books and stuffed them in my bag. Elena came over to me, "I hope the trials go well, Jess."

"Thanks, Elena. Keep your fingers crossed for me."

"Will do. See you on the bus in the morning."

I went down to the changing rooms. There were about twenty of us – slightly more boys than girls. Mr Spencer came over to us, and said he thought the track was safe to run on, so he was going ahead with the trials. I went into the girls' changing room, and started getting into my running gear. The door swung open, and in came Harriet. "Oh, it's you!" she said in a nasty tone. "You're not planning to run, are you? Hope you can manage to stay the right way up."

"Shut up, Harriet!" We both looked up in surprise to hear Naomi had overheard, as she had had followed Harriet into the changing rooms. "Save your energy for running, Harriet. Jess, don't let her intimidate you."

"I'm not planning to," I said, scowling in Harriet's direction. "I can stand up for myself."

It was another twenty minutes before I was called for my first trial. I made sure I wasn't in the lane next to Harriet. The first distance was a hundred metres. Harriet took first place, but I was next to last. I didn't mind – the 100 metres had never been my best distance. Soon afterwards we lined up again for the 300 metres. This time it mattered, and I came in first!

"Not bad, Jess," said Mr Spencer. "It looks like you received some good training in your old school. Congratulations: you've qualified to be in the team!"

Harriet was also chosen, but, sadly, Naomi wasn't

this time. Mr Spencer said he would like her to be a reserve and attend fixtures, to which she agreed.

That evening it was late when I arrived home. I was exhausted and just had to chill out. The living room was empty so I sat down in an armchair. It was over a week since I'd started at my new school and I felt settled. I'd made several friends in class now, as well as Naomi and Aidan. Miss Grant was great, and apart from an over-fussy English teacher, the rest of the teachers were OK, too. I was no longer worrying about coping with physics and chemistry, and even maths was beginning to make sense. The only cloud in my bright blue sky was Harriet. It was like being back with Alice and her buddies.

Why do I attract trouble makers? I sighed to myself, as I scrolled through the TV menu. I was still musing on this when Auntie Joan came through from the garden.

"Ah! I thought I heard the door go," she said. "Your mum's taken Brendan out on his bike. Can I get you a drink, Jess?"

"Thanks, Auntie Joan. I'd love an orange squash, please, but maybe I should be getting you one?"

"I'll put the kettle on while I'm in the kitchen, then you can make me a pot of tea. Then we'll be quits!"

113

Auntie Joan returned in a few minutes with my orange. "I'm curious to know how you're getting on at your new school," Auntie Joan said, "but remember what I said before, you don't have to divulge secrets."

"I don't think I've got any secrets yet. School's been great. I thought I'd miss my old school in Gillingham, but actually I'm happy at the new one."

"I'm glad to hear it, Jess. So, no problems, then?"

twenty

Auntie Joan Confides

No problems? Auntie Joan asked me in such a way that she caught me off guard. I sensed she wasn't meaning to pry, but was giving me permission to get anything off my chest. I wouldn't have told Mum, cos I wouldn't have wanted to worry her, but it somehow seemed safe to share things with Auntie Joan.

I hesitated and then said, "To be honest, Auntie Joan, there is one thing that's bothering me."

"If it's anything I can help you with, dear, I'd love to do so."

"I don't know that you can help, but the fact is that in my old school I was bullied by a group of girls. Now the same thing's happening with a girl in the new one."

"Isn't there a teacher who could sort it out?"

"Perhaps, but I feel I'd rather tackle it myself," I said.

"And how do you plan to do that?"

"I don't have a plan, yet, but I shall get my own back on her one day. I can hear the kettle boiling, Auntie Joan. I'll make your tea." While I was waiting for the tea to stand, I tried to think how I could get even with Harriet. I poured out Auntie Joan's cup of tea, then carried it through to the living room.

"I've been thinking about what you said," said Auntie Joan.

"And?" I asked.

"Jess, if you'll allow me, I'd like to share a little bit from my own life."

"OK."

"I must have been about fifteen years old. Both Sybil and I played the piano. Although she was two years my junior, she could play much better than me."

"That must have been really annoying," I said.

"Very," agreed Auntie Joan. "In fact I was quite bitter about it. Mother would heap praise on Sybil, and always seemed to compare me negatively with her. Sometimes we played duets on the piano, but Sybil always had the best part."

"So you were jealous."

"Both jealous and bitter."

"What did you do about it, then?" I asked.

"I sulked and I brooded for weeks; it might have been months. Then I hit on a plan – nothing complicated, just nasty."

I laughed. "I can't imagine you being nasty, Auntie Joan!"

"We all have the capacity to do bad things, Jess."

"So what did you do?"

"Well, it was harvest festival time. A concert had been arranged in the church, the day after the harvest thanksgiving service. I've told you Sybil was a better pianist than me, but there was one thing I could do that she couldn't. She couldn't play by ear; she always had to have the music."

"And she got the best part in the concert?" I said.

"Yes, it was a part of a Chopin piano concerto, with several complex sections. She practised it for a few weeks before the night, till she had it off perfectly."

"I think I can guess what you're going to tell me," I said. "You hid the music."

Auntie Joan shook her head. "It pains me to think about it even now, but it was worse than that. I burnt it in this very fireplace an hour before the concert. So there was no time to replace it."

I was gobsmacked. "You burnt it? Were you found out?"

"Oh, yes. My father was livid. I wasn't allowed to go to the concert. Fortunately, there were several

117

other performers. I went without dinner for three days running."

"Did Sybil ever forgive you?"

"That's why I'm telling you this story, Jess." Auntie Joan stopped, and I could see that her eyes had filled up with tears. She pulled her handkerchief from the sleeve of her dress and dabbed them. She continued, "Sybil was very upset, naturally, but the very next day, she said that she had completely forgiven me."

"Did you believe her?"

"Yes, but I still held on to *my* grudge until two weeks before she died. She was very weak, coughing all the time, and her chest racked with pain. When I finally admitted that I was wrong to have persisted in my anger and bitterness, and asked her forgiveness, she just put her arms around me – she was bed-bound by then. She hugged me tight, and we both wept for many minutes."

"So you were friends at the end at least."

"Yes, but what a waste! I waited until the end of her life to be reconciled with her, and I only had her as a friend for a fortnight and she was gone." Once more Auntie Joan wiped the tears from her eyes.

"So," I said. "You are telling me that I shouldn't be bitter against bullies, and shouldn't seek revenge."

"Yes, Jess, that's exactly what I'm telling you, because when you're bitter, the only one who's really getting hurt is you yourself."

"But that's hard, if people keep doing nasty things to you. Auntie Joan, I think I know where this conversation is going. You go to church on Sundays and all that, and I know it says in the Bible that we should turn the other cheek, but I'm afraid that when someone does something bad to me, it's in my nature to retaliate."

"Jess, I'm not trying to preach at you. I'm only too aware of my own weaknesses. The bit about turning the other cheek was something Jesus said. Left to myself, I'd be just like you, but Jesus can help us to forgive others. He died for us, and rose again, so we can be forgiven, and then forgive others."

I grimaced. "To be honest, Auntie Joan, I don't think I can swallow that. Sure, Jesus said some good things, and did miracles and helped people, but I don't believe the bit about him dying and coming back to life again. I don't think he's around in the twenty-first century, so I don't think he can do anything to change me."

"I can't prove to you that he's there, Jess, but I can tell you that he changed me from being the angry, selfish person that I was, to being someone who could both receive and give forgiveness. From my own experience, as well as what the Bible says, I would say Jesus is very much alive."

"Well, what do you suggest that I do about the bully at my school?"

"I would encourage you not to retaliate, Jess. Any time she plays a nasty trick on you, try not to think of getting your own back. Even try to think of something you can do to help her, or a little kindness you can show her."

"Help her?" I nearly laughed out loud. "That's not fair! She shouldn't be allowed to get away with being a bully!"

Auntie Joan just nodded. "There's one last thing I want you to know, Jess. I'm praying for you, and for your mother and Brendan, too."

"I don't know how prayer works, or even if it does," I said.

"I don't know *how* it works," Auntie Joan said with a smile, "but I've proven to myself again and again that it does." She paused, and, smiling at me, said, "Now let's see if there's anything worth watching on the television this evening, shall we?"

twenty-one

Athletics Meeting

A couple of weeks later there was an athletics meeting against another Sittingbourne school. The only bad thing about that, was that Harriet was on the team. If only it had been Naomi instead of her!

In fact, Naomi had been off school for two days with a heavy cold, and wasn't even coming as reserve, so I didn't even have her for support.

Harriet couldn't resist goading me when she got on the team bus in the school car park. "I trust you remembered to put on one left and one right foot this morning?" she asked in her usual sarcastic tone.

"Very funny, I don't think," I said. I thought about Auntie Joan's challenge to meet nastiness with kindness, and just managed to restrain myself from saying something nasty back.

The other school's changing room facilities were

shabby compared with ours, but the girls in the other school were polite and made us feel welcome. I was lacing up my left shoe, when the lace broke. *That's annoying,* I thought. I checked the lace. It looked as if it had been cut half-way across. I tied a knot in it; it was a bit short now, but it would do.

As I walked out on to the track I saw Harriet was smirking. *I bet Harriet cut that lace when I wasn't looking,* I thought. Anger surged up and I looked the other way.

As usual I competed in the 200 and 300 metre races. I didn't come first in either, but I recorded a good time in the 200 metres. Harriet came second in the 100 metre sprint, and was first in the under-fifteen 75 metre hurdles. She didn't say anything, but I could see she was proud of herself. I did all I could not to demonstrate any jealousy, though I was feeling it. I couldn't help thinking about Auntie Joan and her sister.

Harriet and I were both in the under-fifteen relay. I was in second place, and as I passed the baton to Harriet I was tempted to make it look as if she had fumbled the hand-over. I resisted the urge, and we won! The other school won the competition overall, but only by a narrow margin.

Travelling back to our school in the bus, I forgot Harriet, and felt a glow of contentment. Running was what I was born for! When I was striding out in a race I was in my element. It was great to think that there was something I was good at.

When I arrived home the sound of piano music floated through the open door. I followed the sound to the dining room. It was the first time I had heard Auntie Joan playing. I stood in the doorway and listened to her; it was a complicated piece of music with fast and slow sections.

"What were you playing, Auntie Joan?" I asked, when she had finished playing. "It was amazing."

"It was part of the Chopin concerto that Sybil prepared for that harvest concert I was telling you about."

"I thought you said she was more talented than you?"

"She was, and now I'm older, I'm making even more mistakes!"

"Doesn't it make you feel sad when you play it?" I asked.

"Quite the opposite, Jess. I imagine Sybil here with me. I feel that if she really was here, she would be encouraging me to play it. It's like acknowledging that we're the best of friends, and take pleasure in one another's accomplishments."

"I wish I could play like you," I said.

"There's plenty of time for you to learn, but you already have things you are good at, like your running. Talking of which, how did you get on today?"

"I didn't win any of my individual events, but we won the relay. The other school won the competition by three points."

"Not bad for your first meeting, then?"

"No, but the girl I told you about is in the team, and she's constantly being nasty."

"And did you respond?"

"No, I managed to restrain myself," I said. I decided not to tell Aunt Joan about my momentary desire to cause Harriet to drop the baton.

"Good." Auntie Joan smiled, getting up. "Jess, there's a bit in the local paper about that cockfighting business. The paper's on the coffee table, if you'd like to have a look?"

We both walked through to the lounge, and I picked up the paper. "Have they caught the gang yet?"

"No, but the police have reported that they've been active again; this time it was just outside Faversham. They keep moving around."

"We had a discussion about it in our social studies class," I said, scanning the article. "Cockfighting has been going on for centuries, apparently."

"Yes, it was banned in Britain years ago," Auntie Joan affirmed, "but I believe the practice is still common in other countries."

"Our teacher says that some people go from this country to France, just to attend cockfights."

"Oh dear, that's terrible," said Auntie Joan, "but the thought that it's happening near here is even more dreadful."

"Perhaps we can help the police to catch the people that are doing it," I said. "Surely there's something we can do?"

twenty-two

Chat with Mum

Are you going to give the club a try, tonight?" Aidan asked me, not for the first time. Elena had been off school all week with bronchitis, and Aidan's bike needed repairing, so he'd sat beside me on the Friday afternoon bus back from school.

"I'm not sure. I've got a bit behind with course work. I've got a history assignment and the English essay to hand in on Monday."

"They've forecast rain for tomorrow, so you're not going to be able to go out much. You could do homework then," Aidan persisted.

"You're not going to give up, are you?" I said. "All right I'll give it a try." I didn't say it to Aidan, but I decided that if I went once and didn't like it, I wouldn't ever go again. "What time does it start?"

"Seven."

"OK, I'll be there," I promised.

When I got home, Mum was preparing a stir-fry for dinner, which was one of my favourites, so I gave her a hand in the kitchen. "How many green peppers shall I chop up, Mum?"

"One should be plenty," Mum replied. "Had a good day?"

"Yes, we had double French this morning. Miss Grant is really nice. She's even making me wonder whether I'd rather teach a language than sports."

"You're what I'd call an all-rounder, Jess. As long as it's a subject you enjoy, I'm sure you could make a success of teaching anything, and you're the sort of person who would inspire others. This move was just what you needed to give you a bit of confidence."

"Thanks, Mum." I gave her a hug. I'd been a bit anxious as to how things would go at the new school, but Mum was right, I was already doing better than I ever had at my old school.

"There's a programme on protecting elephants in Africa tonight," Mum continued. "I thought you might be interested in watching it."

"I would, but I've told Aidan I'll go to the youth club."

"Oh, OK. Good. I'm glad."

"I'll give it a try this once. If I don't like it, I won't go again."

127

"You'll love it," Mum said. "You like being sociable."

"How about you, Mum? You don't really have any social life now."

"Strange you should say that, because Sophie rang up this afternoon. She's invited me to dinner next Wednesday evening."

"You accepted, I hope?" I said.

"Yes, I did. I'll prepare a casserole for you all before I go. Sophie's driving over to take me there. She's curious to see our cottage."

I went quiet, and Mum noticed. "Jess, you're missing your father, aren't you?"

I sighed. "Yes, I suppose I am. I still hate the way he treated you, Mum, and all of us, but I do miss him. He's the only dad I've got – or had, whichever it is."

"I can't say I've forgiven him, but if you or Brendan want to see him, that's all right by me."

"Do you think he'll keep away from the drink, Mum?" I asked.

"I don't know. Alcohol addiction is a powerful thing, and once you've developed it, the urge to drink never leaves you."

"I would still like to see him. Do you think Auntie Joan would let him come here?"

"Probably, but I'd rather he didn't. I would prefer it if you met him on neutral ground. Perhaps we could arrange for him to meet you in Sittingbourne, or something like that?"

"I think I'd like to do that."

"Well, first things first; we need to get this stir-fry finished, or you'll be late for the youth club."

twenty-three

Youth Club

It was raining hard when I left, so I borrowed Mum's umbrella. The church hall door was open when I got there, and I walked in rather nervously. I was wondering what I'd let myself in for.

Aidan spotted me as soon as I got inside. "Hi, Jess! Great to see you! You already know Mike from school, but come and meet the rest. Sarah, come and meet Jess! She's in my class at school and she's come to live in the village."

Sarah, a pretty girl with short brown hair, and a couple of black lads, Christopher, and Marcus, came over and said hi. There were about ten young people in the hall. A group of boys playing pool looked up. I recognised several of their faces from seeing them in the village or on the school bus. They seemed friendly, which was a relief.

Aidan said, "I'm just finishing this game of table tennis with Sarah. Then I'll give you a game, if you like."

I stared a bit when I saw the vicar coming in from the kitchen area. I'd never actually met a vicar before, but he seemed like a normal person, except that he was really tall and wore a shirt with a dog-collar.

"Welcome, Jess, I'm Andrew," he said, seeing me standing there. "Aidan said you'd probably be here tonight. Can I get you a coffee?"

"Yes, please," I replied. I was a bit surprised to be on first name terms with the vicar already. I followed him to the small coffee-bar in one corner of the room.

"Have a seat here," he said, indicating the chairs. "Do you know Amelia and Yinka?" Two girls were sitting opposite on a blue sofa, looking at a magazine. I recognised Yinka.

"I've seen you on the bus," she said. "You're in Aidan's class, aren't you?"

"Yes, I am."

We talked for a few minutes until Andrew came back with two mugs of coffee, which he put down on a low table. "So, tell me a bit about yourself," he said to me, sitting down. His smile set me at ease.

"I moved to Millhurst about a month ago," I began. "From Gillingham."

"Ah, yes," Andrew said, "You've moved in with your Auntie Joan, is that right? And you have a younger brother?"

"Yes, Brendan. I hope Auntie Joan hasn't said too many bad things about us!"

"Not at all," the vicar replied. "She's been most complimentary! Not that your aunt is likely to say bad things about anyone. She always sees the good in people."

"I didn't really know her before," I said, "but coming to live here is one of the best things that's happened to me."

Andrew smiled warmly. "We're all very fond of her in the village," he said. "So what are your interests, Jess?"

"I like running and swimming. I'm in the school athletics team."

"Really? That's great!" he said. "I used to be an athlete myself when I was at school. My height gave me quite an advantage. I've always enjoyed running."

"That's like me; I'm quite tall for my age. Do you still run?"

"Yes, I do the parkrun on Saturdays, plus the local half marathon most years. Well, I'd better let you join the others. As you can see there's pool and table tennis, or you can just sit and chat. We get together for an epilogue at eight forty-five."

"A what?" I asked.

"An epilogue – it's a short talk on a theme from the Bible, and then we open it up for discussion if anyone wants to contribute anything."

I smiled back. I just knew there would be a religious bit! In the meantime I enjoyed playing table tennis. I played against Mike first, and later in the evening with a girl called Grace. She wore very thick glasses, that reminded me of Auntie Joan's. She was brilliant, and won the first match 11-5.

Later, I sat down on a sofa beside Sarah. "Do you go to the Christian Union at your school, Jess?" she asked.

"I'm not even sure if we have a Christian Union," I said. "I've never heard of one."

"We have one at ours," Sarah said. "We meet on Wednesdays after school. One of our teachers is a Christian and he often leads it. At other times one of the students takes it. We choose a topic each week, or watch a video and then discuss it. Sometimes we have an outside speaker. Our vicar, Andrew, comes once a term to speak."

I raised my eyebrows, thinking that didn't sound like a very exciting way to spend part of a Wednesday evening. Trying to be polite, I asked Sarah, "What kind of things do you discuss?"

"All kinds of subjects," she said. "This term we've talked about Should you have a church wedding?, Is it ever right to have an abortion?, and How does a Christian choose a career? Things like that."

"I can't see that choosing a career is any different whether you're a Christian or not," I said, "unless you decide to be a vicar or a nun." Honestly, I was thinking, these Christians bring religion into everything.

"When we discussed it," Sarah said, "we decided that when you were trying to work out what career to follow, as well as thinking about what you're suited for, and what the careers advisor says, we should also pray about it."

I tried not to laugh. "How does prayer help?"

"When we pray, it gives God an opportunity to speak to us."

"You don't hear him, do you?" I asked her. I didn't mean to sound rude; everyone's entitled to their opinions.

"No, he doesn't speak with a voice you can hear, but I believe he does guide us. It might be through a Bible verse, or reading a book, or a friend."

"Or the careers advisor," I said, unconvinced.

"Or the careers advisor," Sarah agreed. "God is not limited as to how he works, but he does listen to us when we pray."

"Don't you find going to church a bit boring?"

"I don't always understand everything, but often the things we're learning about seem to be so relevant to what I'm thinking about or going through at that time."

I was relieved when people started putting chairs round in a circle. I wasn't looking forward to the epilogue, but I'd had enough of listening to Sarah, so I was happy to get up and shift a few chairs. We arranged them in a circle, and everyone including Andrew sat down.

When everyone was quiet he said, "First of all we want to welcome Jess. We hope you enjoy living in Millhurst, Jess, and we're delighted to have you join us at the youth club."

I gave a non-committal smile. "Thanks."

"Two weeks today we're going on the youth weekend at Maidstone," he continued. "All of us who went last year enjoyed it. I need to know by next Friday who's coming, so we can arrange lifts." There was a bit of a discussion about who was going, then Andrew began the talk.

"Tonight I wanted to tell you a story that came out of the Far East; I can't remember which country, but it might have been Laos. A group of farmers, who were Christian believers, were being victimised by some unbelievers in their area. They started re-directing the irrigation system so that all the water went on to their

135

fields, instead of those of the Christians. They did this several days running. The Christians could have thought of a way of getting their own back. Instead they decided to pray about the situation. After that they hit on a plan. They got up an hour early and went into the fields before the others were awake. Then they watered the fields of their enemies. When the unbelievers arrived, they found their morning's work was already done. They were completely taken aback by the Christians' action, and later some of them became believers, too.

"The Bible is talking about just this kind of situation when it says that we are not to take revenge into our own hands, but to leave it to God to sort out. It goes on to say something very strange, that when we return bad deeds with kindness it's as if we pour red-hot coals on the other people's heads. Now, I don't think that means that we are to be nice to people who are unkind to us, just so that they can suffer later. I think it's more like the situation of those peasant farmers – the unexpected kindness of the Christians bowled them over, and caused some of them to change for the better."

It wasn't just those peasants in the Far East who were gobsmacked. Just like Sarah had said, it was as if Andrew knew exactly what was going on my life, all the bullying I was experiencing at school, and my desire for revenge. How could he have known that? Had Aidan picked up on it and told Andrew? Had Auntie Joan told him? Or was Sarah right? Could God be speaking to me through Andrew? Was Jesus really alive and able to relate to us in some way today? Or was I just surrounded by Christians – they seemed to be popping up everywhere in my life – and I was being imperceptibly brainwashed?

Andrew closed the session with a prayer, and then everyone was moving the chairs back. "Well did you like it, Jess?" Aidan asked, as we got our coats.

"I. . . I think so," I mumbled. Honestly, I wasn't sure what I thought. So much seemed to have taken place in the short time since I'd moved to Millhurst. Some good things had happened – Mum was happier, my new school was better than I'd expected, I'd been picked for the athletics team. Yet why was I the one that was always bullied? And I was surrounded by Christians; but what was a Christian anyway? I'd always thought it was someone who did good things for others? Was it more than that? Was it not that at all? As I was leaving the hall, my head was a mass of confused thoughts.

I was glad to have the walk home alone; I needed some space. I needed to get back to my room, talk it all through with Rodney. I put up the umbrella, and headed out into the rain.

twenty-four

Bullying Again

"Good morning, Jess," said Auntie Joan. "You're looking a bit sleepy this morning!"

It was Monday morning. Auntie Joan and Mum were sitting at the kitchen table. I had put off completing my geography project until Sunday evening and it had taken much longer than I'd expected. My alarm had woken me up way too soon.

"Yes, I'm feeling pretty shattered. I was up late finishing off a project," I said.

"I've put your cornflakes in a bowl, Jess," Mum said.

"Thanks, Mum," I said. "Would you pass the milk, please?"

"What's your project about that you got so engrossed in it?" asked Auntie Joan.

"Erosion and expansion along the coast of Kent and Sussex," I said, "and how the coastline has changed over the past 150 years."

"The gales we had last month gouged out huge chunks of the Sussex cliffs," Mum said. "I saw it on the television, but you'd better eat your breakfast or you'll be late for the bus."

I nodded as I slurped my coffee.

"I've been thinking, Jess," Auntie Joan said, "My old bike is out in the shed. I never use it any more; it's slightly rusty, but nothing much. We could get it repaired, and you could use it on the days you stay late for athletics practice, so you don't have to wait an extra hour for the next bus. Or if you want to go off and meet friends at the weekend. What do you think?"

"Thanks, that would be good," I replied, swallowing. "Would it cost a lot to mend it?"

"I don't think so. It probably needs oiling and some new tyres, but not a lot more. I'll see if I can find someone in the village who can fix it for us."

"Thanks," I said. "Gotta dash. Have you seen my shoes, Mum?"

"Where you left them, by the back door." I hurriedly put on my shoes and coat, grabbed my bag and project folder and ran down the lane towards the bus stop.

On the bus I chatted to Elena about music, then the subject of the youth club came up. "Did you enjoy it?" said Elena.

"Yes, mostly. They were all very friendly."

"Aidan's tried to get me to go," Elena said, "but when I asked him about it, he said the vicar usually gives a talk. I'm not into that sort of thing."

"I know what you mean," I said. "The vicar did speak at the end of the evening, but, to tell you the truth, I've been thinking about what he said all weekend."

Elena raised her eyebrows. "Really? What did he say?"

"He was talking about whether we should retaliate when people hurt us."

"Ah, so you've been thinking about Harriet?"

"Exactly, it's as if the vicar knew what I've been going through."

"Just a coincidence."

"Probably," I admitted, "but both my auntie and a girl at the club have been talking to me about God being able to speak to us, and I'm beginning to wonder if it's true."

Elena grinned at me. "Really? I hope you're not going to go all religious on me!"

"Well I want to know what's true and what isn't," I said. "That's all." And we went back to discussing music, then had to run in to school because the bus was late.

Elena needed to see a teacher about something, so she dashed off and I was on my own in the cloakroom...then in walked Harriet. My heart sank.

"Look who's here!" she scoffed. "If it isn't the great athlete herself!"

"Why do you keep picking on me?" I asked. Then Harriet grabbed my project folder, and made for the door. I reached out to snatch my folder back, and she elbowed me sharply in the stomach. I lost my balance, and fell, catching my forehead on the radiator.

"Oh, I am sorry!" said Harriet, holding up my project, and deliberately ripping the first page, before chucking it back at me. "Oh, dear it's torn. Will that matter, do you think?"

She burst into laughter and ran off. I tried not to cry from the pain in my forehead. Slowly I rose to my feet, and picked up the project, feeling a bit dizzy. Not only was the front page of my project torn, but the rest of it was creased. It looked a mess, and I'd spent ages on it. It was due in that day, so I'd have to show it to my geography teacher. I dusted myself down, and went to look at myself in the mirror. My hair was a mess, and a bruise was starting to come out on my forehead. I was furious with Harriet. The cloakroom door opened. It was Naomi.

"Hi, Jess," said Naomi. "You're late! Had a good weekend?" Then she saw my forehead. "Jess, what happened?" she screeched. "Did Harriet do this?"

I nodded and told her everything.

"You can't let this continue, Jess," she said. "Let's go right now and report it to Mrs Streeter."

I was confused. I wanted to do what Naomi had suggested. It was the obvious thing to do, and yet somehow even that seemed like retaliating.

"No, I don't want to tell on her, Naomi."

Naomi caught sight of the spoiled project. "Well you're going to have to explain what's happened to this!"

"All right. I'll tell Mrs Phillips that someone has deliberately damaged it, and ask her for time to print it out again, but I'm not saying who did it."

"I think you should tell everything. Anyone else would."

"No, leave it, Naomi, but thanks all the same."

Later that morning when I showed my project to Mrs Phillips, she was puzzled that I wouldn't name the person who'd damaged my work, but agreed to give me more time. At lunch break Naomi, Elena and I sat at the same table. Naomi was seething when she caught sight of Harriet laughing with her friends, with sly looks in my direction, and she admitted she felt like going over and challenging her herself, but once again I asked her not to intervene.

Changing the subject, Elena turned to Naomi and said, "Jess went to the village youth club on Friday. You go to church, don't you, Naomi?"

"Yes, I do. Did you enjoy it, Jess?"

"Actually, I did. In fact, I'm thinking of going again."

"There's a local youth weekend at Maidstone, the Friday after next," said Naomi. "A group from Millhurst went last year."

"Oh! Yes, they're going again, the vicar announced it," I said in surprise. "Are you going, Naomi?"

"Yes, there's a few of us going from my church. You must come, it'll be fun!"

"I hadn't thought of going till now," I said, "but if you're going. . ." The fact that Naomi was going to be there made it seem a very safe thing to try out. Ever since the meeting on the Friday night I had been turning Andrew's words over in my head. I wanted to know if this Jesus thing was real.

"You have to come!" she said again.

"Well there's no athletics on that weekend, so there's nothing to stop me," I said. "How much does it cost?"

"I'll see if I can find the leaflet."

"I think I'd like to come," I said. "I'll ask Mum if she can afford it."

twenty-five

Business Woman

"Is that you, Jess?" Mum called. She'd heard me come in the front door.

"Yes, where are you?" I called back.

"In the kitchen – I could do with a hand preparing your dinner."

"OK!" I hung up my coat, and joined her in the kitchen. A delicious smell was wafting through. Mum was putting a lid on a casserole dish. "Wow, that smells amazing," I said. What do you want me to do?"

"Turn the oven on, please," she said. "It's chicken casserole. Put it in when the oven's come up to temperature. It needs to cook for an hour. The potatoes are peeled but you'll need to do some carrots. Put them on about twenty minutes before you want to eat. There's yoghurt in the fridge for after."

I bent down to set the control knob on the cooker. Mum noticed the bruise on my forehead. "Oh, Jess, how did you get that knock?" she asked.

"I slipped and fell this morning," I replied. "In the cloakroom, against a radiator."

"You need to be more careful," she said.

"I know. I hope you have a good time with Sophie and Keiran. It's time you had a night out."

"I'm looking forward to it," she said. "Make a change."

"Don't worry about us," I said. "We'll manage to look after ourselves."

"Jess, while you're here, I'd like to talk to you about something else. Auntie Joan has come up with an idea."

"Another one!" I exclaimed.

"The old post office in Millhurst has been closed for a few years, and it's up for rent."

"You're not thinking of us moving, are you?" I asked. I was settled at Auntie Joan's, and didn't even want to contemplate the upheaval of another house move.

"No, but Auntie Joan has come up with the thought that I could open it as a cake shop. It's a bit of a risk, because these days small shops have a job to compete with supermarkets, but if I was to make special, home-baked bread and cakes, it might take off."

"Wow. Your cakes are awesome," I said, "but how would you afford the rent? What Auntie Joan is paying you wouldn't be enough, would it?"

"She is proposing to help with the rent on the shop for the first year, and then, if I'm making enough profit, I'll be responsible for it after that."

"What about cleaning the house?" I asked. "Who's going to do that?"

"If I close the shop for two half-days a week, I think I can manage, especially if you and Brendan will clean your rooms and help out at weekends. Auntie Joan says she'd be willing to serve in the shop for one morning a week. She said she'd only be gossiping to a lot of the customers from the village anyway."

"Well," I said, "I'm stunned. But you said you'd always wanted to run a business, so I think you should go for it, Mum."

"I'm going to think about it. And now I should be getting myself ready, or Sophie will be here."

Next morning at breakfast, Brendan and I quizzed Mum about her visit to Sophie and Keiran.

"What did you have to eat?" Brendan asked, buttering yet another slice of toast. "We had loads of good stuff when we were on holiday."

"Roast lamb with sauté potatoes," Mum replied.

"What are sauté potatoes?" he asked.

"You cut some small potatoes in half, par boil them, and then finish cooking them in butter," Mum said.

"What did you have for pudding?" I asked.

"Strawberry trifle topped with Cornish clotted cream."

"That sounds yummy!" said Brendan, "I wish I could have gone."

"It was really nice. We talked about the shop. Keiran says he's willing to help."

"Oh! I didn't know he could cook," I said.

"Not that kind of help," Mum said, "He's made a very generous offer."

Brendan looked up. "Is he going to give you some money?"

"Not exactly," Mum replied. "When I told them about opening the cake shop, he and Sophie looked at each another, then Keiran announced that he would fit a new kitchen, right up to all the latest health and safety standards, for free! I'd only have to pay for the actual units. Which would halve the cost."

Brendan and I sat there with our mouths open. "That would save loads," I said.

"It would," Mum agreed.

"I was amazed that anyone would think of doing it for me," Mum continued. "Keiran reckoned he could get hold of a discontinued line of kitchen units quite cheaply from the wholesaler. I asked him, what if the shop doesn't succeed?"

"What did he say?" I asked.

"He said it was a risk he was willing to take, and that after I'd told him about the different cakes I make, he judged it to be a small risk. He said I could end up with a big clientele."

"What's a clientele?" asked Brendan.

"The customers," I said. "So did you say yes?"

"At first I refused. I said it was too much, but they insisted. In fact, I think they would have been hurt if I hadn't accepted, so I agreed. Keiran's willing to start as soon as we've signed a contract with the owner of the shop."

"That was an exciting evening for you, Mum," I said.

"Yes, but there was something else, which, if anything, surprised me more than Keiran's offer of helping with the cake shop."

"What was that?" asked Brendan.

Mum dropped her voice a bit. "It concerns your father. I didn't know, but Keiran has been seeing your dad."

"Our dad?" I repeated in surprise.

"Yes," Mum said. "Your dad's been working at a project in Rochester where they restore and sell furniture. Keiran sometimes helps there on Saturday mornings as a volunteer, when he's not too busy with his business. He met your dad there."

"That's a coincidence," I said, starting to clear the table. "What did Keiran say about him?"

"He said that your father is managing to keep off the drink."

"That's good," I said.

"Keiran reckons he's a changed man, and is very sorry for how he treated me," Mum continued.

"Are you going to have him back, then, Mum?" Brendan asked, looking hopeful. "Could he come to live here with us?"

"I'm not ready for that, Brendan, sorry, love. People who drink too much alcohol can stop drinking for a few weeks, or even months, and then suddenly go back to it." She wiped her eyes, and I walked round to her, and gave her a hug.

"So do you think you might take Dad back later, if it lasts?" I asked.

"We'll have to see, Jess. Like I said, I'm not ready to commit myself to anything just yet. But," Mum added, "I think that the two of you should see your father. I've got the phone number of the shop where he's working, and I'd like you to arrange to see him."

"Thanks, Mum. Like you said before, we could meet in Sittingbourne, at McDonald's or something."

Brendan nodded. "Cool. We haven't seen Dad for ages. And I love McDonald's. We could have burgers, Jess!"

twenty-six

Youth Weekend

Andrew had hired a minibus to transport the youth group to the venue for the weekend, which was held in a church hall just outside Maidstone. I was nervous and excited at the same time, as I climbed into the minibus. Had I been too quick to agree to spend a weekend with this group of young people, many of whom seemed very certain about what they believed? I was still not at all sure that God even existed. Was it merely coincidence that since I'd arrived in Millhurst I was surrounded by Christians?

Sarah was on her own near the front of the minibus, and as it was the only seat free, I sat next to her. Aidan was sitting in the next row back. I could tell by the grin on his face that he was pleased I'd decided to come.

On the way, Sarah filled me in on the format of

the weekend — it sounded fun — loads of activities. I couldn't wait to go swimming! Even sleeping on the floor sounded fun. "Last year two of the boys pretended to be ghosts one night," said Sarah. "They thought they'd scare us!"

"Perhaps we can think of a way of getting back at them this year?"

Sarah laughed. "Good idea! We all have to give a hand with the chores, as well. Things like peeling potatoes, and washing up, but when you do it in a group, it's more fun than at home. There are some young people coming from Gillingham this year, that's where you're from, isn't it? And of course there's the talks."

"Yeah," I said, suppressing my feelings of misgiving.

It took about twenty minutes to reach the church hall. It was an old building constructed of corrugated iron, painted green. I'd never seen anything quite like it. Inside it was roomy, though, with big arched windows. Off to one side there was a separate room for the girls' sleeping area, a kitchen, showers and cloakrooms. Sarah and I carried our bags into the girls' room. Naomi's group had been there for a while, and Naomi had already sorted out her air bed and sleeping bag, and propped her teddy bear on her pillow.

"I could have brought Rodney!" I said, seeing her teddy.

"Yeah, you should have done, then they could have had a good chat when we're out!" Naomi's group helped us girls from Millhurst sort ourselves out, then Andrew called, "Supper's ready!"

Andrew, and a youth worker called Freya, from Maidstone, were leading the weekend. Three older ladies from the church, whose hall we were in, were doing the cooking. After baked potatoes, sausages and beans we gathered round the fireplace where there was a log fire blazing.

After an ice-breaker game, where everyone had to introduce themselves as if they were a celebrity, which was fun, Andrew introduced Freya. She was young, with bouncy black hair and sparkly eyes. "Welcome, all of you!" she said. "The group from Gillingham have phoned to say they've had a breakdown en route. Hopefully they'll be here soon. Anyway, this weekend we're going to be looking at a Bible story that some of you will be familiar with: the story of the Good Samaritan. Jesus told this tale in response to a question from a legal expert standing in the crowd. He asked Jesus, 'What must I do to have everlasting life?'"

Just then the door of the hall opened. The minibus from Gillingham had made it! "Sorry," their group leader said, as they all bundled in with their bags and sleeping bags and pillows. "Our van broke down almost as soon as we'd started out, and we had to wait for the breakdown man to come and fix it."

I turned round to see the group of about eight boys and girls come in. I recognised one of the lads who used to be at my old school. There was also a girl with long dark hair who looked about my age.

"Just leave your things on the side," Andrew said to the newcomers. "A big welcome to our Gillingham friends! Freya has started the talk, so take a seat. We've kept you some supper, so you can have it afterwards, though I don't know what it will be like!"

When everyone had found a chair, Freya continued. "We're thinking about the story of the Good Samaritan. It started with someone asking Jesus how to discover the way to eternal life. Jesus did what he often did; he quoted the Bible. He said we were to love God with all our heart, and all our strength, and all our soul, and all our mind, but he didn't finish there. He added, *and to love our neighbour as ourselves*. Which of those commands is hardest, do you think?"

"I'm not sure what Jesus meant when he said that we are to love God with all our heart," I said, "but I think it's harder to love our neighbours, especially when they do cruel things to us." Naomi was sitting next to me, and gently squeezed my hand.

"I think there's a lot of truth in that," agreed Freya. "It's easy to say we're loving God in a kind of airy-fairy way, because we can't see him. To love our neighbours is often a struggle for many of us. God, of course, has shown us what love is, by sending Jesus to die in our place. Love means to put others before ourselves, which is what Jesus did. Now he wants us to go and do the same."

Cheryl, a petite, dark-haired girl, spoke up, "But when Jesus says we are to love God with all our heart, and all of our mind, does that mean we have to give him everything – money, time, ambition – all of it?"

"Yes," Freya said, "and, just as importantly, not take it back again. Loving God is a very practical business. It's easy on a cosy weekend like this to say that we are going to give everything to God, but when life gets tough it can be a different matter. Anyway," she added, looking at her watch, "we'll leave it there for tonight, but over the weekend we're going to be looking at more of what's involved in God loving us, us loving God, and us loving our neighbour."

She said a prayer to close the session. The group from Gillingham quickly made up their beds, while their supper was being heated up. I wasn't on washing up duty, so had some free time. I grabbed a chair and sat looking into the log fire which had now turned to red embers. Once again, the talk seemed to be just for me. Was Jesus speaking to me? Did he really love me and die for me? I decided to try the prayer thing, under my breath. *I don't know if you really exist, Jesus, but if you do, and you are speaking to me, I think I need to get to know you, because I can't forgive the Harriets that keep spoiling my life, without your help.*

Freya must have sensed something of what was going on in my head, and sat down next to me. "I'm not going to intrude on your thoughts, Jess," she said, "but if there's anything you want to talk about or share, I'm here all weekend for you."

"Thanks," I said. My eyes were starting to brim with tears. "Thanks," I managed to say again, and forced a smile. For the second time that evening someone squeezed my hand.

It took me a long time to get off to sleep that night. I could hear Naomi, Sarah and the other girls in the room breathing regularly, but my thoughts were anything but regular. I remembered Isobel, my old school, and the mean Alice Davies and her friends.

I thought of my new school in Sittingbourne, of Miss Grant, of the good friends I had found in Naomi and Elena and Aidan. Then I recalled Harriet's spitefulness, and the day she tore my project. I thought back to that first evening at the youth club, to Sarah's insistence that God could speak to us today, to my own incredulity, and Andrew's talk about the farmers in a

157

Far Eastern country who forgave people who didn't deserve it, and how that story had challenged me. Now the weekend's theme was God loving us, loving God and loving your neighbour. Did God love me? Was Jesus real? Could I ever forgive Harriet, and mean it?

At last, exhausted, I fell asleep.

twenty-seven

A Game of Rounders

I woke to the sound of people laughing. Naomi and Sarah were already up and dressed. I lay for a few minutes listening to everything before I shuffled out of my sleeping bag, and went to the bathroom for a quick wash before getting dressed.

"Hi, Jess," Cheryl said, as I surfaced. "Would you help me lay the tables, please?"

"Sure," I said, with a yawn, and picked up a heap of cutlery. Sarah and Naomi were helping the ladies in the kitchen, preparing scrambled egg on toast. The dark-haired girl from Gillingham was arranging the boxes of cereals. "Hi, I'm Jess," I said, as I laid out the cutlery.

"I'm Parvinder. Someone said last night that you used to live in Gillingham? I moved to Gillingham in September."

"Yeah, I moved to a village near Sittingbourne in August."

"I don't suppose you know an Isobel, do you?" asked Parvinder. "She told me about a Jess who moved."

I stopped and stared. "Isobel's my best friend! We phone each other most days!"

"I'm in her class!"

"Wow, that's amazing! Isobel told me about a new girl. She didn't tell me you were coming this weekend though."

"I told her I was going away for a youth event, but she probably wouldn't have guessed it was the same one that you were going to."

Sarah emerged from the kitchen. "Breakfast's ready. We need to get everyone to come and sit down. Here, Jess, use this saucepan lid as a gong. That should get their attention!"

I banged the lid with a big spoon. The rest of the young people, together with Andrew, Freya, and the Gillingham leader, came into the main hall.

Andrew prayed before we started eating. It reminded me of Auntie Joan. After breakfast, Andrew gave a little talk on loving God with all our being, and his love for us. I kept thinking of what Cheryl had said the previous evening about putting our ambitions at God's disposal. I had lots of them – I wanted to do well at school, maybe become a teacher. I dreamt of excelling at athletics – maybe not the Olympics, but running for Kent, at least. Then I had ambitions for Mum – the cake shop to be a success. And I had one final ambition for myself – I wanted Dad back, but not drinking any more. God's list of ambitions for me might be totally different, and that would be too big a price to pay.

I tried to focus on what Andrew was saying. "God is no man's debtor. We can not give more to him than he gives to us. If we surrender our money, our time, our will to God, he gives us much more in exchange. I'm not saying that if we give God £5, he will necessarily give us £20 back, but whatever he does give us will be worth more to us than anything we've forfeited."

More than success in athletics, I wondered, *or enjoying being a teacher, or seeing Mum happy?*

After breakfast we piled into the minibuses to go swimming. It was the best fun ever, with flumes and a wave machine, waterfalls and a whirlpool. I hadn't been swimming for months, and I'd almost forgotten how much I loved it, although we didn't do a lot of actual swimming! I got to know quite a few of the other young people while we messed about, and we hardly stopped laughing the whole time.

I sat next to Aidan in the minibus on the way home. "You enjoying it so far, then?" he asked.

"Yeah! Swimming is one of my favourite things ever, but I feel something of a fraud even being here. I'm still not totally sure that there is a God."

"But you hope there is," he said. "Don't you?"

I had to think about that. "I'm not sure, but suppose I did, does that mean I can just imagine him into existence, because I want him to?"

Aidan grinned. "No, if anything, his existence is more real than yours or mine!"

"I wish I had your faith," I said with a sigh. "It would make things easier."

"I don't know that I've got a lot of faith, either," Aidan said, "but perhaps how much faith we've got is less important than using whatever faith we do have. God is the one who gives faith. I think faith is like using a little key to open a big door."

I didn't have time to think about that for too long, cos we were back, and it was lunchtime. Soon we were sitting down to eat cottage pie and peas, followed by raspberry tart and cream.

While we were still at the table, Freya stood up. "While you're finishing your meal, we're going to think about the next bit of the Good Samaritan story. That's loving our neighbour. As Jess said last night, that sometimes seems harder than loving God. In another part of the Bible it says, 'If you don't love the person

162

whom you can see, how can you claim to love God whom you can't see?'" I nodded. It made sense.

Freya continued, "Whoever this person was who was quizzing Jesus that day, he was bold enough to ask Jesus the second question, 'Who is my neighbour?' That prompted Jesus to tell the story about a man who was on a journey, but as he was on a lonely bit of the road he was beaten up, robbed, and left for dead. A Jewish priest and a temple official, who you'd think would have gone to his rescue, walked past. It was left to a Samaritan, someone who would have been despised by the Jews, to take pity on this unfortunate traveller. It's one thing to help our friends, but this story shows us God even expects us to help our enemies."

I was shocked: it was exactly what Auntie Joan had said. Help our enemies – not just forgive them? Me *help* Harriet? I couldn't get my head round that.

Yet, once again, it was as if Freya knew what was going on in my mind. The more she said about going out of our way to be kind, even to people who are unkind to us, the more I felt it wasn't Freya speaking to me at all, but another voice; someone who knew exactly what I was thinking. Could it be God? It wasn't a blaming kind of voice – more like he wanted to – I don't know, set me free. I don't think I can explain it any better than that.

Freya had stopped speaking. She was praying, and once more the words seemed to match exactly where I was. I could feel something happening, deep down in my soul.

"Wash-up team," Andrew announced, "it's over to you, now. After you've finished, it's out to the field for some games."

When we got outside, there was a stiff breeze blowing, but the sun shone brightly between the clouds that were racing across the Kent sky. Aidan and Cheryl had been appointed the two team captains for the first game: rounders.

"I want Jess on my team," Aidan said, "She's the fastest runner."

"In that case I'll have Naomi," said Cheryl. "She's almost as fast as Jess."

Our team was first in to bat, and we played well. We notched up an impressive score before we were all out. Then I took up a fielding position quite close to the batter. Cheryl was the second one to bat for her team. Aidan bowled. Cheryl took a mighty swipe and whacked the ball really hard. I wasn't quick enough; the ball caught me straight on the right knee. A terrific bolt of pain shot up my body and I fell to the ground.

Not again! I thought. *First my shoulder, then my head and now my knee!*

twenty-eight

Encounter

Cheryl and Naomi helped me up, but it was difficult putting weight on my right foot because of the pain in my knee. I squealed as I stood up.

"I'm soooooo sorry, Jess!" Cheryl said, bending over me.

I tried to smile, but tears came to my eyes and I winced with the pain. "Don't worry, it wasn't your fault. I shouldn't have been standing so close."

Cheryl and Naomi helped me limp back to the hall, and Freya ran to get a cold compress. "This will help stop the swelling," she said, pressing it to my knee.

"I'll sit with you," said Naomi, "Cheryl, why don't you go back and play? Then the teams will be even again."

"I feel awful," said Cheryl, "going back to play, when I've injured Jess."

"Honestly, it's fine," I said. "I'll be all right in a few minutes." My knee continued to throb terribly, but the cold compress was soothing.

"This is the second time that Naomi has had to pick me up off the ground," I told Freya, after Cheryl went back to the field.

"Oh! When was the first?" Freya asked.

"She was set on by a girl at school, and nearly knocked herself out on a radiator," Naomi said.

After a slight pause, Freya asked, "Are you being bullied, then, Jess?"

"There's this girl in the athletics team..."

"I'm sorry to hear it."

"You know, Freya," I said, "when you were talking about loving our neighbour this morning, I kept thinking about her."

"In relation to God telling us to love our neighbour?" Freya asked.

"Yes, although if you'd asked me yesterday, I'd have said I wasn't sure if there was a God."

"And now?"

"And now, I just feel that God, or maybe it's Jesus, is saying to me that he's seeing everything that's going on in my life. It's like – he understands."

"Jess, he does understand. It sounds like Jesus is doing something very special in your life right now. He loves you more than you can know. We have been thinking about giving God everything this morning – receiving his love is the only way we can love other people. Do you think you're ready to open up your life to God?"

"I think so," I said, "This morning I was struggling with the thought of giving him control of everything, especially my ambitions. But I do think he's there."

"Jess, any plans God may have for your life are much more wonderful than anything you could possibly devise yourself, or even hope for. And you're right, he is there. Here, in fact!"

"I think I do believe, now, that God is there, and that he cares, but I don't think I'm going to make a very good Christian."

Freya laughed. "It's not like that, Jess! None of us do. We all mess it up, but like Naomi did for you, God is good at picking us up again and setting us on our way – or rather his way. It's a journey that will take us all the way to heaven! If you are ready to ask Jesus into your life, and to let him take control, then I will lead you in a simple prayer."

"I'd like that," I said. "Do you think I should, Naomi?"

"If you think you're ready?"

"I think I am."

"Well then, Jess," said Freya, as we all smiled at each other, "If I pray, do you want to pray after me?"

I nodded, my knee almost forgotten. Then Freya said a short prayer, a phrase at a time. I can't remember the exact words, but basically I was saying sorry for all I had done wrong, and asking Jesus to forgive me and help me to live my life his way.

"You may not feel any different right away..." warned Freya, after we'd all said Amen.

"But I do feel different!" I said. "I feel like a weight has been lifted off me!"

"That's great!" said Freya, and Naomi gave me a big hug.

Freya warned me though, "It won't always feel like that; there will be plenty of ups and downs, but what you said is exactly right, Jesus is with you, and he will always be with you. Now is there anything else we can do for you, or would you two girls like some time on your own?"

"Actually, would you mind asking Aidan to come over?" I asked. "I want him to be the first person to know I've become a Christian."

twenty-nine

Meeting Dad

Dad was already sitting at a table against the back wall when we arrived at McDonald's in Sittingbourne the following Tuesday evening. He looked a bit tense, but got up and waved as soon as we went through the door.

"Hi, Dad!" yelled Brendan, running over to him. "Oh, you look strange with a beard; Jess said you'd started growing one."

"Does it suit me?"

"Looks great!" Brendan said. "But I might need to get used to it a bit."

"You've changed, too – you've grown taller since I last saw you."

"My new shoes are size four!"

"Hi, Jess," Dad said, turning to me.

"Hi, Dad," I said, and gave him a hug. "Have you been waiting for us long?"

"My bus came a while ago so I've had a coffee. Shall we order something to eat?"

"Have you got enough money, Dad?" I asked, "cos I've got some pocket money..."

"No, it's fine, I earn a bit doing some jobs, and I've got some vouchers," he said, "but thanks anyway."

Brendan went to the counter with Dad. I could hear Brendan telling him some of his corny jokes, and I could see Dad relaxing a bit. He and Brendan carried the trays to the table.

"I've brought chocolate milkshake for you, Jess. Brendan said that's what you'd want."

"That's great, Dad, thanks."

Eating a meal with Dad, after such a long time, and without Mum, seemed odd at first, but Brendan chattered on about football, which helped.

"How's your new school, Jess?" Dad asked, when Brendan paused for breath.

"It's great, and I've made several good friends. I've made the athletics team, too."

"Well done, Jess, I'm so proud of you. And how about your school, Brendan?"

"I love it," he replied, stuffing fries in his mouth like they might disappear if he left them there too long. "We get to do more fun activities like nature walks."

"Dad," I said, "Dexter's dad told Mum that you're not drinking any more. Is that right?"

"Yes, Jess. I've not touched it for three months now."

"You're cured then?" I asked.

"Perhaps. The truth is that the temptation to go back is always there. Sometimes it's a real battle walking past a shop where they sell alcohol."

"Perhaps it's a bit like running," I said. "Once you've run a distance in a certain time, you know you can do it again. So when you have to go past the shop, tell yourself that you managed to walk by the last time."

"You're right, Jess, but it's still not easy. You must think your father's a failure."

"No I don't, Dad," I said. "You've got a problem, and I keep hoping you'll get over it, but you're only a failure if you stop trying, so Miss Grant told me when I failed a French test the other day."

"Sometimes I feel like you don't need me any more," Dad said. "I'm the one that should be providing you with a home. Now you've settled in with your mum's aunt, you don't need me any more."

"Don't say that, Dad," said Brendan, hugging his arm. "It's not true! I miss you loads, and I want you back living with us again."

"Thanks, son, but I don't believe your mother's going to have me back. What I'll do, is work hard and get a place of my own, then you can come and visit me. How does that sound?"

We both nodded. "Mum might change her mind, though," said Brendan, and I nodded again.

"Dad," I said, "For once, Brendan might be right, if you can stay away from the alcohol. We love being with Auntie Joan, but we still want our dad. Don't we, Brendan?"

"Yeah, we do."

Dad smiled. "I've brought something for you both. Here, Brendan, this is for you." He passed a large plastic bag to Brendan.

Brendan looked in the bag. "Wow, Dad, a football! Next time we see you, can we go to a park?"

Dad smiled and nodded. "Maybe. This is yours, Jess. It's not much, but I made it myself."

I took the small package, wrapped in brown paper. I unwrapped it, and inside was a beautifully polished wooden goblet. "I didn't know you could do that, Dad," I said in surprise.

"At the furniture restoration shop there's a lathe, and the supervisor is teaching me wood-turning."

"It's awesome," I said, and meant it. "I'll put it in the middle of the shelf over the fireplace in my bedroom. Something to remind me of you."

"I think of you two every day," Dad said. "I'm sorry not to be seeing much of you, but it's great to see you're both happy. What time is your bus back?"

"There aren't many buses in the evening," I said, "so Auntie Joan said she'd meet us outside in the car park at half seven."

"That's in ten minutes," he said. "It's seemed such a short time together."

"We'll have to go to a park next time, though, Dad, yeah?" said Brendan again. "Play with my new football?"

Dad ruffled his hair. "Sure, son, we'll do that."

"Dad, before we go," I said, "There's something I want to tell you."

"Good news, I hope?"

"Very good news. Dad, I've asked Jesus into my life. I've become a Christian."

"You look happy on it," he said.

"I am. Whatever happens, I know Jesus is there with me."

"It was only last weekend, but already she doesn't moan at me so much now," Brendan said, wiping his mouth with his hand. I handed him a face wipe and we grinned at each other and high-fived.

Dad smiled, too. "Jess, I'm pleased for you. I haven't sorted it all out, but my supervisor goes to church, and he says Jesus can help me with the drink problem."

"Wow, Dad," I said, "I can't believe it! Suddenly God is everywhere! You know what, I'm going to start going to church, and I'm going to pray that Jesus does help you."

"Thanks, Jess," Dad said, and I could see he had tears in his eyes.

"You must come and say hi to Auntie Joan," I said, desperately holding back my own emotions. "I think she'd like to meet you again."

"After all she's heard about me from your mother?"

"Auntie Joan always seems to see the good in people," I said. "You'll like her."

"I haven't seen her since the day your mother and I got married. I've even forgotten what she looks like."

We went outside. Auntie Joan's old car was already in the car park. When she caught sight of Brendan and me walking with Dad, she got out and came to meet us.

"I'm Trevor," said Dad, holding out his hand. "It's years since we met."

Auntie Joan shook his hand warmly. "You have two children to be proud of, Trevor," she said.

174

"I only wish they had a father they could be proud of."

She smiled. "They both love you a lot. You know, sometimes children can be a lot better at forgiving than us grown-ups."

"Thank you for giving them a home," Dad said. "I wish there was some way I could repay you, but there isn't."

Auntie Joan smiled. "Actually, I asked them to come and live with me because I needed the help at home, so there's no repaying to be done, I assure you."

There was a bit of an awkward silence, then Dad gave me and Brendan a hug, and turned and strode away.

thirty

Isobel Visits

"Rodney, you'll have to sit on my pillow so that Isobel can have the chair," I said, moving him over to my bed.

"Ooh! He's looking rejected," Isobel giggled, as I propped Rodney up in a comfortable position next to Bernard, who stretched and yawned.

"Parvinder was full of the youth weekend that you spent together," Isobel said.

"You'll have to come next year!" I said. "I really liked Parvinder. She said she'd settled in well at school."

"She invited me round to her house last week," Isobel said. "Her mother's a really good cook. Everything was spicy, but it was amazing."

"It's great you've become friends."

Isobel pouted. "It makes up a bit for you leaving."

"I miss you, too, but at last you've come over for the weekend! It's so great you've finally made it! You know what you said about going for a country walk? One of my new friends from the village, Aidan, has arranged for his mum to give us a lift to a place near Cheapstone tomorrow, which Aidan says is a good place for a walk. He knows the route so we won't get lost."

"Is it far from here?"

"No, just a few minutes in the car. His mum's going to drop us off at the start of the walk. It goes through some fields and woods, apparently."

"So it's just the three of us going?" Isobel said.

"No. Brendan was feeling left out, and Mum said we should let him come."

"It'll be fun," Isobel said. "I love the country. I can't believe this view from your window!"

"Wait till you see it in daylight. You'll like Aidan. He helps his dad on Saturday mornings, so we can't leave until about twelve tomorrow, but we're taking a packed lunch."

"Sounds like you've made a lot of friends in the short time since you moved," Isobel said.

"Yeah, but you're still my best friend, Isobel. Hey, that's Mum calling; she's got dinner ready. She's made pasties – they're the best!"

The next morning I forgot Isobel was sharing my room, and nearly stood on her! We stayed in bed till late, messing about in our pjs and catching up with everything, but we were ready by the time Aidan arrived with his mum in their little green car.

The sun was shining – it was the best day ever for exploring the country. Mum had made us a massive bag of sandwiches, and Jennifer had made another batch of muffins, which Aidan had brought with him.

As Mum waved goodbye, she called out, "Jess, don't leave Brendan out of what you're all doing! And Brendan, be good!"

"I won't," I called back, just as Brendan yelled, "Course I will," and we high-fived as we squeezed into the back of the car.

A few minutes later we'd arrived at the gate that led to the start of the walk. Aidan and I got our backpacks out of the back of the car, and Jennifer drove off with a wave.

"Wow," said Isobel, as the sound of the car's engine faded into the distance. "This is awesome!"

We all agreed it was. It was so peaceful – the caw of birds, the wind rustling the branches of the trees, the autumn leaves changing into all their amazing colours. It was such fun to be out on our own, too, especially with Isobel.

"We go along this short path through the trees," said Aidan, climbing over the gate and jumping down the other side. "Let's go!"

"The adventure begins!" I agreed, and we all grinned at each other.

"I've brought my catapult," Brendan said, jumping down from the top of the gate. "I'm going to hunt for a rabbit."

"Just make sure you're aiming well away from us then," I warned.

The path wound its way under a group of smooth-barked trees which had lost most of their leaves. The ground fell away to the left and there were numerous rabbit holes. I couldn't see Brendan catching one, but trying would keep him out of mischief!

Beyond the trees the route opened out into a large sloping field. The path went down at an angle towards the left-hand corner of the field, where we came across a herd of black cows. As soon as he saw them, Brendan stopped dead. "I'm not going through that field – it's full of bulls!"

"They're not bulls," Isobel assured him. "Even I can tell a bull from a cow, and I live in the town."

"All the same," I said, "I'll be happier when we're well past them, in case they take an interest in us and run down towards us."

It was fine, although we took nearly fifteen minutes to cross the field, especially as we had to keep stopping while Brendan showed us how good he was with his catapult. He'd decided bushes were easier to shoot at than rabbits, which were keeping themselves underground anyway, safely out of trouble.

The next field, over a stile, sloped gently downwards, with a wood running along its bottom edge. The sun came from behind a big grey cloud, and Isobel and I decided to sit on a log and soak up the rays.

"I don't want to just sit, I want to keep on going," Brendan complained.

"Let's go up to the top of the field then," Aidan said to him, "and we can have a competition aiming at the fence posts." This pacified Brendan, and the pair of them set off happily.

"Good job we're not relying on you to supply us with a meal, Brendan," I shouted after them.

"You wait," Brendan called back. "I'll get better and better, and catch three rabbits."

From where we were sitting we could see the wood below us. There seemed to be a stream running through it because we could see a bridge way back to our left. Beyond the woods the fields sloped up quite steeply.

"I'd love to explore that valley later," I said.

"I'm trying not to be jealous of you," Isobel said, "living in this beautiful countryside. I'm getting all kinds of ideas for writing adventure stories."

"Are you still writing, then?" I asked.

"Yes. Most of my stories are about horses, of course. One day I'm going to have my own stables, you wait, and a library, where I'll write my books."

The sun was shining on her black hair. I could picture her as a princess being rescued by a handsome prince on a grey and white dappled charger.

"Trouble!" I said, turning round to look behind us, "The boys are on their way back."

"Hey, Jess," Brendan called out breathlessly, "I'm getting better! I can hit the fence posts nearly every time now!"

"He's doing well," Aidan said, coming up. "Maybe next time he really will catch a rabbit!"

"I'm hungry," I said, "Shall we have lunch now? After that I'd like to check out the stream down there."

"Great idea," Aidan said. "Come on, Brendan, sit by me. It's lunchtime."

"Good!" Brendan said, "I'm starving. But I'd like to climb those fir trees at the top of the field after lunch."

"And not come with us girls on a walk?" asked Isobel.

"I'd rather climb trees."

"Well," Aidan said, "what if Jess and Isobel go down to the stream, and you and I climb trees?"

"That'd be great," Brendan said. "Pass me a sandwich, Jess."

"You're allowed to say *please* even in the country," I said.

"Please," he said, holding out his hand, and I rolled my eyes at him as I passed the bag of sandwiches round, and bottles of water.

As we munched away, Aidan turned to Isobel. "Jess told me you've been best friends for a long time."

"Yeah, since we started school. Our teacher put us on the same table and we've stuck with each other ever since," Isobel replied.

"Shame that you've got separated," he said.

We both nodded and said "yeah" at the same time.

"It's lovely here in the countryside, though," Isobel said. "It'd be great to have Jess living near again, but I can see why she's happy here."

"At least we're not a million miles from Gillingham, and you can get to visit," said Aidan.

"You must keep coming to visit, Isobel," I said, squeezing her arm. "Much more often!"

"I'm bored," Brendan said, after munching his way through a mountain of sandwiches and two chocolate chip muffins. "Can we go climbing now, Aidan?"

"OK," Aidan said. "Shall we swap mobile numbers, in case we need to text?" After we'd got the phones sorted, the boys set off back up the field. "We'll come down and find you in about an hour," called Aidan as they left. "Then we'd better head back to the road, cos it'll be getting dark."

Brendan had gathered a pile of small stones, and was catapulting imaginary rabbits as he went. At the same time we could hear him boasting to Aidan about the high trees he'd climbed in the past.

thirty-one

Caught

"Come on, Isobel," I said, clearing up the lunch rubbish. "Let's find that stream."

Isobel and I picked up our backpacks and set off down the hill. It was fun, just the two of us again. We laughed and chatted about old times as we followed the grassy footpath through a gap in the hedge, then turned left on to a proper path which ran through the woods. We'd been walking for about ten minutes when we started to hear men's voices in the distance.

"We're not alone," Isobel whispered.

"Perhaps it's some other walkers coming," I suggested. We kept walking, but stopped talking as the voices got louder. There seemed to be quite a few men together by the sound if it, and in one place. Suddenly Isobel stopped.

"Something is making me feel uncomfortable," she

said quietly. "I don't know what it is, but there's something wrong about this. I'm nervous. Let's go back."

"Let's see who it is, first," I said. The sun was shining through the trees towards us. "Sounds like they're in the woods. It might be Scouts or something."

There was some bracken between the woods and the stream. "If we creep through the ferns," I said, "we might be able to walk past without them seeing us."

Isobel screwed up her face. "I'm not so sure that's a good idea. I still think we should turn back, and find the boys."

"Well, you stay here and I'll just take a quick look," I said. "I don't see why they should spoil our walk!"

I crouched down, and started to creep forwards. There was indeed a clearing. Several cars and vans were parked there, and a group of men were engaged in a lively discussion about something. Most of them had their backs to us.

Three or four more men were setting up a kind of large fence, or cage. A chicken squawked. With a shock, I realised what I was witnessing. This was the cockfighting gang the police were looking for!

A rush of fear rose up inside me, and my heart began to pound. I needed to get out of there. I'd just turned round to creep back when Isobel's phone rang, really loudly. I heard her answer, but couldn't make out the words.

Someone else had heard it, too. I heard a shout. "There's someone watching us!"

Next thing, two or three of the men started running in our direction. I sprang up and sprinted back towards Isobel as fast as I could. The bracken slowed me down, though, and one of the men caught up with me and grabbed my arm.

"What are you up to?" he snapped, holding tightly to my wrist. My heart was pounding as I turned to face my captor. He was tall, with a big moustache and smelt heavily of cigarette smoke. I didn't answer, but as I looked the other way I caught sight of Isobel's blue jacket moving away through the trees.

"Right, this way," said the man, tugging me roughly back towards the clearing.

One of the others, a short man, said, "Steve, what are you doing? Let her go!"

"And let her tip off the police? They've been round all the schools telling the kids to contact them if they see anything."

"I don't like this," the third man said. "I agree with Jim, we should let her go."

"Well, I don't," said the man called Steve, who was still gripping my arm.

"There's another one here!" the third man shouted, and ran towards a willow tree just ahead of where we were standing. Someone in a pink jacket and blue jeans stood up, and started running away fast. She had blonde hair. I stared in total amazement – it was Harriet, of all people!

Jim and the third man started to chase her. Like me she was slowed down by the undergrowth. They came at her from two sides, and then I heard her crash to the ground, and cry out. The third man pounced on her. "Got you!" he said, hauling her up.

"Stop, my ankle's hurting!" she cried out. Jim and the other man took one arm each, and led her across to where Steve was holding on to me. All the other men were watching from a distance. And they didn't look friendly.

"Harriet?" I asked. Her face was pale, but she looked defiant.

"Jess!" she said, and even in my shocked state, I sensed it was in a warmer tone than she had used to speak to me before.

"What are we going to do with them, Steve?" the third man asked. He was younger than the other two, though a heavier man.

"I don't know, but I think we need to get away from here, fast."

They led Harriet and me round to the back of the van. Harriet was limping, and in obvious pain from her ankle.

"Jim, you hold on to this one," Steve said, "while I discuss with the others what we are going to do."

He moved towards the fenced-off area, leaving me and Harriet in the grip of the two men. The back of the van was open, and I gasped as I saw there were cockerels in three or four separate cages. One of them crowed at that moment. Me and Harriet exchanged a horrified glance. Steve was obviously one of the leaders, and indicated to the other men to move off a few yards. They must have been discussing what to do about the two of us.

After what seemed like ages, Steve came back.

"I wasn't expecting to get into anything like this," said the younger man, sweating profusely.

"We need to get out of here as fast as we can," said Steve. "The others are dismantling the ring, and going to put it back in my van. We'll tie up the two girls, and get away from here. I told you we should have waited till it was dark. And whoever picked this place, close to a *public footpath*..."

"We can't just leave them here!" Jim said.

"Well we can't take them with us," Steve said. "We'll tie them up, and then call the police from a public phone in about half an hour. That way the police can't trace us."

"I never intended to get into anything like this," the younger man said again.

"Nor did I," said Steve angrily, "But I can't think of another way out of it, can you?"

"No," he replied.

"That's it then," Steve said. "There's a piece of cord in the back of the van. We'll tie them back to back. They won't come to any harm here."

Steve fetched the cord. I struggled as he tied the cord tightly round my wrists whilst Jim held my arms behind my back. Then Steve pushed me firmly down on the ground, and the younger man forced Harriet to sit down with her back to me. She gave a low cry from the pain in her ankle. Then Steve tied up Harriet's wrists, and finally bound us together.

"Jess, don't worry, we'll get out of this," she whispered.

Steve heard what she said, "Not till we're safely away."

"I still don't like this," the younger man said.

"None of us does," Steve said, "but we have to do what we have to do. Now let's be going."

All the men got in their cars and van, then the convoy started up the track that led away from the other side of the glade.

"What are we going to do, Harriet?" I asked, as the sound of the engines faded in the distance. "And another thing, what are you doing here?"

thirty-two

Reconciliation

"I was going to ask you the same question," Harriet said. "What are *you* doing here?"

"I was out for a walk with Aidan Edwards in my class, my little brother and my friend, Isobel, from Gillingham. The boys went off climbing trees, but Isobel and I were walking through these woods when we heard voices."

"What's happened to your friend? Did she run off and leave you?"

"She probably worked out we'd both get caught if the men saw her. I hope she's gone to get help. Why were you hiding by the trees, Harriet?"

"My uncle owns the farm the other side of the stream. I was out for a walk, too, when I caught sight of the vehicles. So I made a detour and crossed the stream further up. I crept up until I could see them. There's nobody here usually, and Uncle Robert hadn't said anything about there being visitors. I half-suspected it might be the cockfighting gang. I had just made a note of the number of the van on my phone, when yours rang and they spotted you."

"Actually, it wasn't my phone, it was Isobel's," I said. "Hopefully she'll get Aidan and Brendan and they'll come and set us free."

"We should be figuring out a way to get this rope off our wrists," Harriet said. "We can't just sit here and wait! I'm getting cold!"

We tried, but soon gave up. The cord just cut into our wrists every time either of us moved. "It's no use," I said. "Every time we move, the rope cuts in deeper. We'll just have to wait to be rescued." For a minute we sat in silence, then it started to dawn on me how incredible this all was.

"Harriet," I said, "this is so weird! We've been enemies for weeks, and now we're tied together, trying to help each another."

"I was thinking the same thing," she said.

"Why did you take a dislike to me?" I asked.

"You simply happened to be the wrong person in the wrong place."

"What do you mean by that? Why did you need to pick on anybody at all?"

192

"I'm not really sure," Harriet said, "but I was feeling angry."

"With me?"

"No, just life in general."

I frowned. This didn't seem to be making sense. "What do you mean?"

She sighed, and paused before replying. "My father is ill. He was diagnosed with leukaemia five months ago, and, well, the treatment hasn't gone well. The doctors still don't know if he's going to get better or. . . or die."

I didn't know what to say. "That's awful," I managed, eventually.

Harriet's voice sounded wobbly. "I'm scared of losing him," she whispered.

"I don't know what to say."

"There's nothing you can say that will make any difference," she said.

I thought for several seconds before speaking again. "Harriet, I don't want you to take this the wrong way, but I recently became a Christian, and I believe God can make a difference. Even if we don't have the power to change things."

"I don't believe in God," she said.

"I said exactly the same thing till recently."

"It's God I've been most angry with," Harriet said. "Actually, that sounds really stupid when I've just said I don't believe in him."

"Maybe he doesn't think it's so stupid. Maybe he understands how you're feeling better than you do."

"This isn't helping us get free," she said.

"No, it isn't, and that's why I'm going to pray about it right now."

"Do it, if it makes you happy," Harriet said. "Sorry. I didn't mean that to sound rude. And while I'm at it, I'm really sorry for being mean and spiteful to you at school."

"That's OK. And now I'm going to pray. Do you mind if I pray out loud?"

Harriet shrugged, so I did, and I prayed for her dad, too. Harriet was quiet for a minute. Finally she said quietly, "Thank you."

I didn't know what to say next, but then we heard it. "It's a helicopter!" Harriet shouted.

"It's coming right over us! Please see us. Please, look this way!" I begged the helicopter, as the noise drew nearer. It seemed to circle over us for a bit, but then it flew away. "It's gone," I said, bitterly disappointed.

"They must have seen us, surely?" Harriet said. "How could they not have seen us? I hate to say it, but it shows prayer doesn't work." We didn't

194

have long to think about that, because there was a sound of crashing through the undergrowth and Aidan appeared.

"Jess, it's me," said Aidan, panting. "Are you all right?" Suddenly he stopped running and stared, seeing I wasn't alone. "You're Harriet Coutts, aren't you?" he asked in surprise. "What are you doing here?"

"Aidan!" I said, "Am I glad to see you! Are Isobel and Brendan with you? We've been tied up, can you get the ropes off?"

Aidan's jaw nearly hit the floor when he saw our wrists, and he began to untie them as quickly as he could. "The others are fine. I told them to run back to the road to wait for Mum," he said as he worked on the knots. "I phoned her and she's coming straight away. Brendan and me saw everything from up in the trees – the cars and vans and everything! That's why we phoned Isobel, hoping to stop you from getting any nearer."

"Oh, you saw it all. I can't believe you were watching us! And it was you who phoned Isobel?" I gasped.

"Yes, Brendan and I could see everything from up in the tree. We could see the men, the cockfighting ring, and then we saw the men pounce on you, Jess. We moved quick after that. You've got to give it to

Brendan – if he hadn't wanted to climb trees we'd never have seen you."

"Who's Brendan?" Harriet asked.

"He's my little brother," I said. "Did you see the helicopter, Aidan? Was it the police?"

"Yes, I think so. I phoned the police, right after warning Isobel. They're probably chasing down the gang. There, you're free!"

Having the cords off our wrists was a relief, but we were both pretty shocked, and really cold, and Harriet started crying. "I'm sorry, I don't know why I'm crying, I think it's the relief of being free." I sat down beside her and gave her a hug. I was feeling a bit shaky myself.

Then we heard more vehicles approaching. We were poised ready to run, as an old grey truck entered the clearing, followed by a police car with flashing blue lights.

"It's Uncle Robert!" Harriet said.

"And the police," added Aidan. "Oh, and Mum right behind!"

thirty-three

A New Life

"We ought to have hired a music group or something, to play carols," Naomi said, as she pinned Christmas bunting round the shop.

Aidan grinned as he passed her up the drawing pins. "I think that might have been a bit over the top!"

"Still, I think it looks amazing in here," I said. "This is my mum's dream, coming to life." I was holding a tray of doughnuts. "Mum," I called, "shall I put these in the front window, next to the snowman cakes?"

"No," she said coming through from the shop's kitchen, "I want them in the counter display case. You can put this toffee and walnut cake in the front. Wow, you three have done a fabulous job," she congratulated us. "It looks wonderful! Really festive!"

"I'm surprised Brendan's not here sampling the cakes," Aidan said.

"That's precisely why he's been banned," I said, "at least for this morning. There'd be nothing left to sell."

"We haven't got the paper bags out," Mum said, scanning the shop to see what else had been forgotten. "Jess, they're in the two white boxes at the foot of the stairs; there are large and small ones. Bring about thirty of each please."

The cake shop shone with new white paint; the glass and steel display cases were gleaming and the delicious smell of freshly baked bread filled the air. Just five more minutes to opening. I gave Mum a hug along with the bags. "Mum, you must be really excited. I know I am."

Her eyes were shining. "I can hardly believe it's happening. I hope it'll all be worthwhile, and we get lots of customers!"

"Of course we will," I said. "We've pushed five hundred leaflets through people's doors! Great design, by the way, Aidan."

"My first graphics job!" he replied with a grin.

"Right, it's half past eight," Mum said. "Everyone ready? Time to open the door, and, look, Mrs March is our first customer."

Business was a bit slow for the first hour, but then Jennifer came and bought the toffee and walnut cake, and from then on there was a steady trickle of people buying bread, éclairs, mince pies and Bakewell tarts. Aidan left soon after opening time to help his dad, but Naomi spent the whole morning in the shop with me and Mum.

"Anything else need doing, Tracy?" she asked, when we had a sudden lull.

"You could bring in some more white loaves, please, Naomi; the shelf is nearly empty."

Around eleven o'clock, Naomi and I had a coffee break. We sat on a low wall in the little yard at the back of the shop, in the winter sunshine. The smell of baking bread was still lingering in the air.

"It's gone really well this morning, hasn't it?" I said. "Thanks for helping."

"It's been fun. Worth it to see your mum happy."

"Yeah, haven't seen her like that for...I don't know, ages. Will you still be able to meet up at Harriet's uncle's farm tomorrow afternoon?" I asked. "I'll be able to get there on Auntie Joan's ancient bike, now she's had it fixed for me."

"Yes, I'll cycle over, too."

"Harriet's excited about having us all over, now her ankle's better," I said. "It's amazing what God has done. Since we had the counselling and stuff about

199

what happened, she keeps texting me. Her uncle has got a horse which she rides, and she says we can all have a turn."

"Oh, that'll be fun! Have to wear boots then. How is Harriet's dad?"

"They're going to start him on a new treatment. She says the doctors are hopeful he will get better."

"Well, he's on my prayer list," Naomi said, "and Grandma and Grandpa say they're praying for him, too."

"Next weekend Isobel is coming for another sleepover," I said. "I hope she'll come to church with me. Auntie Joan has really taken to her. They both have the same imaginative spirit. Isobel texted to say she'd written another short story, so she's bringing it for Auntie Joan to give her some tips."

"Jess, I can hardly believe it's only three months since you came to live here."

"I know what you mean. My life has changed so much in that time. So many good things have happened. Getting to know Auntie Joan; making new friends, including you, of course; joining the youth club and becoming a Christian; getting into the athletics team at school, busting the cockfighting gang, and now, seeing Mum fulfil her dream, too! She said if it goes well, she'll take Brendan and me on holiday next summer. How amazing is that?"

Naomi gave me a hug. "Jess, there may be ups and downs, but I believe there are lots more good things to come."

We clinked mugs and I grinned. "Here's to my new life!

Reading Group Questions

1. Jess's family is struggling financially. Have you ever wanted something but not been able to afford it? Do you sometimes think life is unfair?

2. Jess doesn't want to move house at first. People talk about *fear of the unknown*. Have you ever been afraid of doing something scary, but it worked out all right in the end?

3. Everyone's good at something. Jess is good at running. What talents do you have?

4. Jess wants to see her dad again, but her mum says she won't take him back. Do you think they both have a point? Do you think there's a difference between forgiving someone who has hurt you, and allowing them to do something bad to you again?

5. At first, Jess wants to get her own back on Harriet, but later things turn round. What do

you think about the way Jess deals with the different incidents of bullying in the story? What would you have done, if you were Jess?

6. Cockfighting is a cruel sport. Jess equates it with being bullied, and wants to do something about it. Have you been prompted to action when you have seen a person or an animal suffering?

7. Jess is initially nervous about getting involved with religious people. She said she didn't want to be brainwashed into believing something that isn't true. Do you think this is sensible?

8. During the weekend away, Jess starts to pray. What do you think about praying? Do you think God hears?

9. Jess becomes a Christian during the story. Her life has already changed a lot, but this changes her from the inside. Do you think this is possible in real life?

10. At the end of the book Naomi says, "Jess, there may be ups and downs, but I believe there are lots more good things to come." Do you think this reflects real life for everyone, or just some people?

Finding God

If you would like to become a Christian, like Jess and Aidan, and millions of people in real life, you need to talk to God. You can do that anywhere, any time.

Here's a first prayer you can use if you like, similar to the one Jess prayed in the story:

Dear Lord,
I realise that my sin has stopped me from knowing you in the past, but I believe you died in my place. I'd like to live my life your way from now on. Please forgive me and send me your Holy Spirit to be with me for ever.
Amen.

If you take this step, make it real by talking to God every day, reading the Bible and going to church, so you can grow in your faith.

If you would like to contact the author about anything you have read in this story, please do so through the contact form on the Dernier Publishing website:

www.dernierpublishing.com

You may also like:

Revenge of the Flying Carpet
by J.M. Evans

Paul's twin sister, Trinity, makes his life a misery. When he finds a magic carpet he plots revenge, but gets a lot more than he bargained for.

"A brilliant, captivating story" - Naomi

"Very engaging. I understood from it the importance of forgiveness." - Reuben

Beech Bank Girls, Every Girl Has a Story
by Eleanor Watkins

The Beech Bank Girls share their laughter, their tears, their hopes, their fears and their secrets with each other and with us. Miracle and party included!

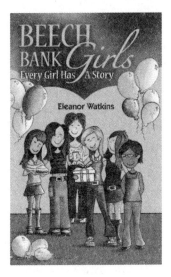

"A fantastic read!" - Natalie

"I loved reading about the different girls' lives." - Emma

The Only Way
by Gareth Rowe

When a miserable, disaffected teenager meets the beautiful and mysterious Lily, he has to risk everything to save his own life, and hers.

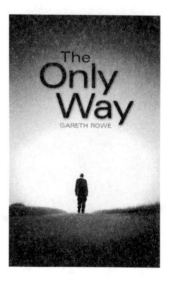

"Really exciting things happen." - Naomi

"This is a very good book." - George

London's Gone
by J.M. Evans

London has been bombed by terrorists. A group of teenagers have to make a hazardous journey to safety. But is anywhere safe now?

"I just couldn't put this book down." - Gilly

"Very exciting, full of atmosphere." - Eleanor